THE LIEUTENANT'S KISS

"Lydia, do not poker up on me," he said, resisting when she tried again to release herself. "I had good reasons for not wanting to meet you this afternoon, but they seem unimportant now. The regiment is leaving soon for Ramsgate. From there we will embark for the Continent. I do not know when I will see you again."

Lydia stopped dead in her tracks and stared at him in dismay.

"I have so many things to say to you," he said earnestly, "and there is so little time."

Yet they spoke very little on the way to Lydia's house because Edward set such a rapid pace that Lydia could not speak beyond a gasp. Threading their way through the traffic took all of their concentration.

A street away from the house, however, Edward startled Lydia by pulling her into his arms.

"I do not think it would be wise for me to walk boldly up to your mother's door," he said softly. He silenced her with a finger over her lips when she would have spoken. "No time for arguments, love. I know one is supposed to lead up to this sort of thing by slow stages but—"

Then Edward kissed her, and the rest of the world just fell away.

Books by Kate Huntington

THE CAPTAIN'S COURTSHIP
THE LIEUTENANT'S LADY

Published by Zebra Books

THE LIEUTENANT'S LADY

KATE HUNTINGTON

Zebra Books
Kensington Publishing Corp.
http://www.zebrabooks.com

ZEBRA BOOKS are published by

Kensington Publishing Corp.
850 Third Avenue
New York, NY 10022

First Printing: November, 1999
10 9 8 7 6 5 4 3 2 1

Printed in the United States of America

To Bob Chwedyk, my wonderful husband.

ONE

Yorkshire
July, 1814

The unladylike shriek of rage that rent the air soon after the arrival of the morning post sent all of widowed Annabelle Whittaker's four remaining daughters scurrying for the parlor.

Since the marriage during the previous month of Mrs. Whittaker's eldest daughter, Vanessa, to Alexander Logan, Lord Blakely, one of the most eligible bachelors in England, a state of unprecedented tranquility had settled upon the household in the absence of its mistress's chronic complaints and fits of the vapors. For weeks Mrs. Whittaker had floated along on a veritable cloud of happiness and optimism, enjoying all the triumph of a matchmaking mother whose wildest ambitions had been achieved.

It was a relief for her younger daughters, in a peculiar way, to have this unnatural state of affairs brought to an end, as end they knew it must. The violence of their mama's emotion made her too incoherent for speech at first, a strong indication of the seriousness of the catastrophe.

"What is it? Mama, *speak* to me!" cried fourteen-year-old Mary Ann. She and her younger sisters, Amy and Agatha, crowded around their mother in alarm.

The last to arrive on the scene was Mrs. Whittaker's second

eldest daughter and the only one who could do anything with her mother when she was in this state.

Lydia, a sensible young woman of seventeen years, knew there was only one person who could cut up her mother's peace so completely.

"What has horrid Uncle Henry done now?" she asked calmly.

Mrs. Whittaker looked up at her daughter, started to speak, then burst into another tirade of passionate tears. Lydia plucked the letter from her mother's limp grasp.

"What is it?" asked Mary Ann, trying to look over Lydia's shoulder.

"It appears," said Lydia, frowning, "that horrid Uncle Henry is evicting us from this estate. Our cousin Edward is about to set up his household and Uncle Henry intends to give him this one. Immediately. The wretched man! He would do so after we have gone to all the expense of the spring planting."

"I wanted to go to Brighton for the summer," Mrs. Whittaker said reproachfully, glaring at Lydia, "but, no, *you* insisted that a trip to a fashionable resort would be a shocking waste of money, and we must take most of the revenue from the rents and put it back into the land. Now we have nothing. Nothing!"

"Well, Mother," Lydia said with a tight-lipped grimace, "it appears you were right after all."

"I do not understand, Lydia. Can he evict us in Mama's lifetime?" asked Mary Ann.

Lydia looked up from the letter.

"I am afraid so," she said. "The estate is entailed property, so Uncle Henry could have evicted us any time after Papa's death. He has permitted us to live here thus far, he says, from proper family feeling."

"Proper family feeling, my eye, just as if he did not throw his so-called generosity in my face at every opportunity!" Mrs. Whittaker snapped.

"True," Lydia said, looking up from the letter briefly before she continued reading. "But now that Mother has found a rich son-in-law, he intends to wash his hands of such improvident relations. I must say this letter is most eloquently phrased, deplorable though it may be in content. Lady Margaret must have had the dictating of it."

"That Woman," Mrs. Whittaker said in accents of loathing worthy of Mrs. Siddons. "Do not speak of *her."*

"Believe me, no one wants to speak of Lady Margaret, Mother," Lydia assured her. "Uncle Henry, disagreeable though he may be, could never hope to approach the genuine maliciousness of his lady wife."

"Dreadful woman!"

"Dreadful, indeed. I have never understood why she hates us so much," Lydia said, turning her attention back to the letter. "Uncle Henry wants possession of the house on Friday next, at which time he expects Mother to give him an account of her 'stewardship,' as he is pleased to call it."

"We will be forced to live on the street, begging our bread!" cried Mrs. Whittaker.

"We will do nothing of the kind," Lydia said coolly. "Mother, it is not helpful for you to say such things in front of the children. See, they have begun to cry again. Never mind, darlings. You know Alexander would never permit us to live on the street." She smiled at the younger girls. "On the other hand, it does sound exciting, does it not? We should have to teach you how to pick pockets," she added, and was rewarded with a pair of teary giggles.

"I could dress in men's clothes and rob coaches," offered Mary Ann, getting into the spirit of the thing.

Mrs. Whittaker gave her daughters a look of deep reproach for this unbecoming levity. Lydia wiped the smile off her face and patted her mother's shoulder.

"Do not worry, Mother. All will be well, I promise you. Horrid Uncle Henry *would* insist that we leave the house before Alexander and Vanessa have returned from their wedding trip. It is most awkward to have to ask Alexander to provide us with a roof over our heads less than a month after he has married into the family."

"I *refuse* to be here when Henry comes to claim the estate," Mrs. Whittaker said belligerently. "Give him an account of my stewardship, indeed! No doubt he means to rip up at me for every bit of unplowed ground and broken fence!"

"If so, he has a great disappointment in store for him," Lydia said placidly. "Do not fret, Mother. When Uncle Henry comes, he will find you, the girls, and our personal property gone. I will stay and prepare the house for him. I am far better able to answer his questions about the way the estate has been managed than you are, and I would positively relish the opportunity to give him a piece of my mind."

Mrs. Whittaker looked at her daughter with mingled respect and disapproval.

"I sometimes marvel that I could have given birth to a daughter with so little sensibility," she said.

"So do I," Lydia agreed with perfect cordiality. "Have you realized, Mother, that when we leave this estate we will never have to speak to him or Lady Margaret again?"

"I had not thought of that," Mrs. Whittaker said, looking almost cheerful.

"In the meantime," Lydia said, "we have much to do."

She faced her sisters with all the assurance of a general. With her usual efficiency, she had already worked out the details of their removal from Yorkshire.

"Mary Ann, you and the girls can occupy your time in packing your clothes while we are waiting to hear from Alexander. Take the girls up to their room and help them determine which things still fit them and which should be put in a box for the parish."

"Yes, Lydia," said Mary Ann, taking her little sisters by the hand and leaving the room.

"There," Lydia said with satisfaction. "That should keep them busy for the rest of the day. Mama, you and I shall go through the house and determine which furnishings you would like to keep."

Mrs. Whittaker put her hands on her hips.

"I refuse to leave behind the new velvet draperies we bought for the parlor before Vanessa's wedding."

"I have kept the old ones in a cupboard and we can put them up again," Lydia said, sitting down at her mother's writing desk and selecting a pen. "We will begin sorting through things as soon as I dash off a letter to Alexander. With luck we will have a reply by the end of the week."

As it turned out, Alexander did better than that. Five days later, Alexander and Vanessa swept into the parlor just before dinner time.

"Vanessa, darling!" Mrs. Whittaker cried upon having her favorite daughter restored to her. Vanessa was a very pretty blue-eyed brunette whose cheeks were blooming with happiness and good health. Her tall, dark, imposing husband, Alexander, followed her into the room with his arms full of gaily wrapped parcels. He put the presents on a low table, but Aggie and Amy pelted into the room and practically knocked him over with the exuberance of their welcome before he could properly greet his mother-in-law.

"Girls!" Mrs. Whittaker said, shocked by their unladylike shrieks of delight. "What will Alexander think?"

"Alexander will be vastly flattered that his favorite girls have missed him so much," the gentleman said, answering for himself. "Come along, my dears, and see what we have brought for you from Brighton."

Alexander waited until Vanessa, her mother, and her sisters were occupied with the presents; then he took Lydia by the arm and quietly led her from the room.

Once in the bookroom, he gazed at her in concern.

"Lydia, I was shocked to learn your Uncle Henry has used you so ill."

"So were we, and we *know* him," she said dryly as she indicated a chair at the head of the library table before she seated herself. "It is unfortunate we have to impose on you when you are so newly connected with our family, but I am afraid we have no choice."

"Do not be absurd. You are *my* family now. Vanessa and I have come to take all of you to Brighton for the rest of the summer. I will come back on Friday to deal with your uncle."

Lydia could not help smiling. How like a man. It would never occur to Alexander that the rooms must be cleaned, that provision must be made for the middle-aged husband and wife who served them, that there were still animals to care for, and that someone must arrange to have all of the ladies' possessions conveyed to wherever the Whittakers were to live now that they were forced to leave Yorkshire.

With an emotion akin to panic, Lydia looked at the faded but still beautiful Turkish carpet on the floor and the warm, golden spill of light from the tall window that she used to drowse in like a sleepy cat on winter days when she was a child. She had picked the red roses that graced the center of the table just this morning while the dew was still heavy on them. Next summer Cousin Edward's bride would pick roses from the garden Lydia had tended so lovingly.

Lydia could not bear to think about it. Instead, she made a mental note to have the carpet beaten and rolled up for removal to their eventual home. Her mother always had been so proud of her only Turkish carpet.

"Lydia? Are you listening to me?"

"Certainly, Alexander," she said, shaking off sentiment. "Mama and the girls would enjoy it of all things, but lodging in Brighton is so dreadfully dear! Are you quite certain you want to—"

His part-humorous, part-exasperated look made her smile.

"Yes. I suppose you are," she said.

He gave her a mocking bow.

"I will stay behind and tend to the disposition of the house," she continued. "Uncle Henry will not have the satisfaction of seeing it in less than perfect condition. We must be permitted to have *some* pride, you know."

"Would you not rather go to Brighton at once? I will hire some girls from the village to give the place a good cleaning so it will be ready for its new occupants."

"Heavens, no!" Lydia exclaimed. "One could not expect them to do a proper job of it without careful supervision. I *would* be grateful for the additional help. Mr. and Mrs. Grundy do very well in keeping the kitchen and gardens tidy, but they are getting up in years and I can hardly expect them to do the kind of heavy housework I have in mind."

"You would have done it all yourself, I suppose."

"It would not have been the first time," Lydia said with a shrug of her shoulders.

"Very well, then. I shall see to hiring some girls from the village immediately," Alexander promised. "And I will come back on Friday to escort you to Brighton as soon as the business with your uncle is concluded."

"I would not put you to such inconvenience for the world," Lydia exclaimed. "I could just as easily take the stage from the inn."

"My sister by marriage is not going to travel alone on the common stage!"

When Lydia opened her mouth to protest, he gave her the look that probably had cowed his recruits into immediate submission when he was a captain with Wellington's army.

"Very well," she conceded.

"Indulge me, my dear," he said with a grin. "Having sisters to worry about is a delightful new experience for me. If you think I am difficult to deal with now, wait until Amy and Aggie are old enough to have suitors."

"Amy and Aggie are children," Lydia pointed out. *"I* can take care of myself."

"Certainly," he said, humoring her. "When the summer is

over, you will come with us to our place in the country while the dower house is being made habitable for you. It will need some work because it has not been occupied since my maternal grandfather's time."

"I am certain it will do very well," Lydia said. "I shall get to work on it as soon as we arrive."

"Lydia, *dear,*" he said, patting her arm. "No one appreciates your hard work in caring for your mother and sisters more than I, but you are my sister now and I employ servants to do the scrubbing and polishing."

"I suppose I am to sit on a cushion and sew a fine seam," she said with a sigh.

"That, or anything else you wish," he said. "You will have much to do before your debut."

Lydia rolled her eyes.

"Alexander, I have told you repeatedly that I have no wish to make a splendid come-out!"

"No arguments, if you please," Alexander said. "Vanessa and I have arranged it all between us. Think how much your mother will enjoy launching another daughter into society."

"Can you seriously imagine me wearing white and simpering behind my fan at all the bachelors?" Lydia scoffed. "All of this will cost you a *fortune,* and to no avail, for my matrimonial prospects are decidedly slim."

"Nonsense. The Whittakers are a fine old family, and your mother's people are perfectly respectable. There will not be the slightest difficulty in finding you a husband."

"Oh, certainly not," she agreed wryly. "I am no beauty, and I have none of the accomplishments by which society sets such store."

"Perhaps not, but you are a very pleasant-looking young woman. You have pretty blue eyes and a nice smile—"

"And plain brown hair, and an unfashionably plump figure—"

"And a great deal of common sense," Alexander concluded,

ignoring her interruption. "Any man of reasonable intelligence would be pleased to acquire such a wife."

Lydia gave an unladylike snort.

"I am perfectly serious," Alexander said. "I nearly killed my horses to get to Yorkshire, certain I would find a houseful of hysterical females having the vapors. Instead I find neatly labeled trunks stacked in the hall for removal, the younger girls perfectly cheerful, and your mother clutching her vinaigrette in the parlor but otherwise in better state than I dared hope. You need not tell me whose cool head is responsible for this happy state of affairs."

"You know very well that men look for decorative females with a bit more sensibility in their wives."

"Nonsense! Much as I esteem your dear mother, I am greatly relieved that neither you nor Vanessa are afflicted by her precious sensibility!"

"Ah, Alexander," Lydia said soulfully. "If only there were more men with your enlightened tastes."

"I have friends," he said with a twinkle in his eye. "I will be happy to introduce you."

"I hope you will do no such thing! Your fashionable military gentlemen and rakes about town are much too smart for me. If you can find me a reasonably genteel man between the ages of twenty and eighty who does not gamble or indulge in spirits overmuch, I will be more than grateful. I am not fussy, I promise you."

"I shall keep my eye out for a suitable candidate," Alexander said, smiling. "Shall we join the others now?"

"Certainly. I imagine you are famished from traveling all day. I will just have a word with Mrs. Grundy and join you in the parlor."

Mrs. Whittaker and her daughters set off for Brighton with Alexander and Vanessa the following afternoon, leaving Lydia alone in a house that already looked neglected from having so many familiar objects removed from it.

The first wave of girls would come up from the village in the morning to help prepare the place for its new owners. In a week Lydia would leave the house she had been born in, never to return.

For the first time since horrid Uncle Henry's letter arrived, Lydia had the leisure to take it all in.

Her mother had complained about the house's unpretentious appearance, its distance from London, and the lack of servants to lend her consequence, but Lydia herself had loved it.

Walking slowly so she could memorize every room as she passed, Lydia went to the library and lay on her back in the warm patch of sunlight on the Turkish rug until the darkness fell.

TWO

Edward Whittaker cushioned his pounding head with one hand against the window of the coach and pretended to be asleep in the vain hope that his father would stop blustering. His esteemed parent never tired of impressing upon Edward a sense of his vast privilege and good fortune in being the son and heir of so important a personage as Henry Whittaker, a gentleman with blood so blue that the daughter of an earl was not considered too great a match for him.

It was enough to make Edward wish he had made the journey on horseback, even though that surely would have made his head fall off altogether.

Now all his parents' schemes for Edward's future were about to come to fruition, it seemed. Edward's maternal grandfather, the earl, was attempting to purchase for him a commission in a cavalry regiment. After Edward distinguished himself in his military career and married a suitable young lady from a lineage at least as impeccable as his own, he would justify the major reason for his existence, that of breeding sons to carry on the Whittaker name.

He supposed the military service—like the string of racing prizes that attest to a stallion's virility and endurance—would serve as some sort of credential for his potential as a sire of healthy little Englishmen.

Edward briefly considered casting up his accounts all over

his father in midrant, a fate Henry Whittaker richly deserved
for making Edward accompany him on his shameful errand.
The last thing Edward needed after a night of conviviality on
the town was a jolting carriage ride into Yorkshire at the break
of dawn so he could witness the edifying spectacle of his father
throwing his late brother's impecunious widow out of the house
she had first entered as a bride. His father's enjoyment at the
prospect of this act did him no credit in Edward's eyes. He only
agreed to accompany his father because he wanted to prevent
him from treating Aunt Annabelle and her blameless daughters
with more harshness than was absolutely necessary.

Mr. Whittaker often adopted a belligerent manner when he
was about to do something that disturbed his conscience.

Once his uncle's widow was out of the way, the estate would
be readied for Edward and his prospective bride, the one with
the unexceptional pedigree and large dowry who would make
him the happiest of men when the time was right for him to
provide his father with grandchildren to carry on his name.

Between Edward's parents and his grandfather, the earl, Edward's life was all arranged. No wonder Edward spent most of
the year in his lodgings in London, avoiding his family and
devoting himself to the amusements of the metropolis.

"It will cost me a fortune to put the house to rights," Henry
grumbled. "Annabelle is the most improvident creature, so it is
probably falling down around her ears."

He gave a snort of disgust.

"It was once my father's primary residence," Mr. Whittaker
went on, obviously trying to convince himself that his sister-in-
law deserved her fate, "and I continued to let Annabelle occupy
it after George's death, not that she was grateful. All the little
ninnyhammer would do is complain because her jointure was
not adequate to support her family and provide dowries for her
miserable daughters, as if it was my fault that George gambled
and drank away every shilling he could get his hands on. And
was it *my* fault the silly woman had five daughters?"

"Are we almost there?" Edward asked, perfectly aware that all of his father's questions were rhetorical ones.

"Yes," Henry said. "It will not be long now."

Soon after that, the carriage turned into a narrow country lane lined with recently planted saplings, and pulled up in front of a pleasant-looking stone manor house.

"It will have to be enlarged, of course, when you bring Lady Madelyn here," Mr. Whittaker said complacently, "for you will do a prodigious amount of entertaining."

Edward opened his mouth to voice an objection, but he decided he might as well save his breath. Lady Madelyn Rathbone was the daughter of an earl who had distinguished himself as a general and gone on to a brilliant diplomatic career before sticking his spoon in the wall and leaving his only child a very wealthy young woman. Edward's parents were convinced that she was the perfect wife for him.

Never mind that Edward's acquaintance with Lady Madelyn so far consisted of standing up with her for one country dance at one London ball. As his mother pointed out—much to Edward's disgust—why should it be difficult for a young man to fix his interest with any young lady when he is a veritable Adonis? It had always been a great source of satisfaction to Lady Margaret that her firstborn was blond, gray-eyed, and long-limbed like all of her family instead of dark and stocky like the Whittakers.

Henry heaved his bulk out of the carriage when the footman opened the door. and looked around the grounds, frowning, Edward thought, for the absence of something to criticize. The yard, while obviously not designed by any of the fashionable landscape architects, was perfectly presentable. A profusion of flowers bloomed in the tidy beds flanking the steps to the house, the boxwood hedges were neatly trimmed, and the grass was lush and green.

Edward and his pounding temples were exceedingly grateful that the lane to the house did not contain many ruts.

Henry waited impatiently for his servant to knock on the door, and tapped his cane on the step in annoyance when no one answered right away.

The young woman who finally appeared was dressed in a plain, well-worn gray gown, and her light brown hair and good-natured, dimpled face were liberally coated in dust. Her pretty blue eyes widened when she saw the two gentlemen.

"Disgraceful," Henry huffed in disapproval. "Kitchen maids answering the door. Tell your mistress that Mr. Henry Whittaker and Mr. Edward Whittaker have arrived, girl."

He tried to hand her his hat and cane, but she made no move to take them.

"Are you *deaf?*" Henry demanded in exasperation.

"No, Uncle Henry," the girl replied with some asperity. "Are you *blind?*"

Edward gave his father a look of disbelief. She might be a bit disheveled, but Edward would have thought not even his father could mistake her for a servant. Edward had not seen any of Annabelle Whittaker's children since the funeral of her husband in 1811, but he had recognized Lydia at once. Teasing his feisty little cousin was one of the fondest memories from his youth. He could always depend on her to give back as good as she got.

"Good afternoon, Cousin Lydia," Edward said when his father appeared to be speechless. "If you have an ounce of humanity left, open the door and let me out of this heat or I shall be thoroughly and vilely sick right here."

She stood back at once and allowed the gentlemen to enter, but the shrewd look in her eyes told Edward that she had instantly perceived the cause of his discomfort.

"Burning our candle at both ends, I see," she observed.

"Your tender solicitude touches my heart, cousin," he said, enjoying her sniff of disapproval in spite of the headache. She ignored this comment and turned to her uncle.

"You must excuse my appearance," she said. Her manner

made it clear she could not care less whether he did or not. "The village girls are still cleaning below stairs, and I was supervising them."

"I gave you ample warning of our arrival," Mr. Whittaker complained.

"You said you would come *tomorrow*, Uncle Henry, and you did not mention that Cousin Edward would accompany you. Perhaps you would like to step into the morning room for some refreshments while I see about another room."

"Some strong tea would be just the thing," Edward said hopefully before his father could answer. Mr. Whittaker gave him a quelling frown before he turned back to the girl.

"Where is your mother?" Mr. Whittaker demanded.

"My mother and sisters have gone to Brighton, sir."

"I specifically said in my letter that I expected her to be here!"

"Yes, your letter *did* say that," Lydia said, not in the least flustered by his belligerence, "and a great many other uncivil things besides. You wanted her out of *your* house, and now she is gone. If you wish to ring a peal over someone's head about it, I am quite at your disposal."

Edward would have laughed at the expression on his father's face if his head had not hurt so much. The old man had expected to find a houseful of timid females to bully. Instead he was faced with this remarkably self-possessed, clear-eyed young lady who refused to be intimidated by him.

"Little baggage," Henry complained to Edward after Lydia had fetched them the tea and biscuits and then excused herself. "If the rooms are not fit to sleep in, we will have to go to an inn tonight."

"If you wish," Edward said after he took a large gulp of the tea. It was prepared just the way he liked it, strong and fragrant.

"I imagine it is too much to hope that the sheets are well aired."

Because Mr. Whittaker was facing away from the doorway,

he did not see that Lydia was just entering the room and could hardly avoid hearing this ill-natured remark.

"I think you will find your room adequate, sir," she said, her cool tone belying the spark of anger in her eyes. "You will stay in the master bedroom, of course. Cousin Edward, I have put you in Vanessa's old room. It has the nicest view of the gardens, so you may as well have it."

"Thank you, Cousin Lydia," Edward said, amused by this ungracious speech.

A lady would have pretended not to hear his father's remark, but Edward had to acknowledge that she had been sorely provoked. With the posture of a queen, she preceded the two gentlemen and his father's valet up the stairs and showed Mr. Whittaker into a pleasant room sparsely furnished in some heavy mahogany pieces popular during the previous century. Obviously the furniture that the widowed Mrs. Whittaker meant to take to her new home already had been removed. The room was tidy as a pin.

"We keep country hours, sir, so dinner will be at six o'clock."

Henry gave her a brusque nod of acknowledgment and dismissal. Lydia favored Edward with a smile that did not reach her eyes and led him to his room, which was even more sparsely furnished than the master bedroom. It contained only a bed, a wardrobe, and a small battered chest.

"Papa bought Vanessa a pretty bedroom suite when she was twelve, and when Vanessa married Alexander, Mother gave it to one of the younger girls. This set is sadly shabby, but I assure you the mattress has been well aired and the sheets are clean." She sounded a bit defensive.

"This will do very well, cousin," he said.

"Your fiancée will wish to refurbish the house to her own taste, anyway, I imagine."

"My fiancée?" he asked, taken off guard. "I am not betrothed."

Lydia looked surprised.

"I gathered from your father's letter that you were eager to establish your household here. Is that not why my mother was ordered to leave so abruptly?"

It probably behooved him to fall in with his father's falsehoods, but Edward decided that it was impossible to look into his cousin's earnest face and lie.

"I am not betrothed," he repeated. "My father intends to give the estate to me eventually, but there certainly was no urgency in requiring you to leave it."

"I see," Lydia said, and it was obvious she did. "Well, cousin, I thank you for your honesty. I am surprised Lady Margaret did not wish to be in for the kill."

"My mother was indisposed," Edward said defensively. His mother *had* wanted to be present so she could gloat over her sister-in-law's misfortune.

"Now, *that* is certainly a pity," Lydia said dryly. She looked up when a tired-looking, middle-aged servant entered the room with a steaming mug of liquid.

"Thank you, Mrs. Grundy," Lydia said, taking it from her with a smile and a nod of dismissal. The woman curtsied and left the room. "This should help, Cousin Edward."

"Help?" he asked, regarding the brew with trepidation. It had a peculiar purplish color and there was a bit of grayish froth on top.

"My father was fond of the bottle, too," she said. "I mixed this up and set it on the stove before I joined you and your father. I asked Mrs. Grundy to bring it here when it was boiled."

"What is in it?"

"You do not want to know," Lydia said straight-faced, "but it always made my father feel better." She reached under the bed and withdrew a glistening but slightly chipped white ceramic chamber pot decorated with painted pink roses.

"See here, cousin! Surely that will not be required," he objected.

"This floor was just mopped this morning, so I would prefer that we do not take chances."

"Too kind of you," Edward said dryly. He braced himself and manfully drank the contents down all at once. His eyes watered and he could not restrain a loud, embarrassing belch. But after a horrible moment of upheaval, he found that he did feel better.

Lydia stoically stood at the ready with the chamber pot, and gave a little nod of satisfaction when she realized it would not be needed.

"It . . . works," he said in surprise. He could have wept with relief. "Thank you."

"I will leave you to sleep it off," she said, taking the mug and leaving the room.

What a surprising girl, Edward thought while he removed his boots and stretched out on the bed. Cousin Lydia had made her contempt for her uncle's family perfectly plain, and no one could blame her under the circumstances. His own state of post-drunken suffering met with equal disapproval. Yet she bothered to give him a remedy for the pain in his head and stomach.

As he fell asleep he reflected that whatever else her family's financial difficulties had done to the little cousin he remembered, it had not hardened her heart.

It only had sharpened her tongue, he thought with some amusement.

An hour later he awakened refreshed and eager to be doing something. No matter how badly he abused the bottle, Edward had never been one of those chaps who could sleep the following day away. For a moment he enjoyed the fragrance of roses wafting in through the open window. Then, restless, he went in search of Cousin Lydia's stimulating company.

He found her in the bookroom busily writing at a table. He noticed that she had tidied her hair and changed her clothes. No one would mistake her for a kitchen maid now, even though she was dressed with more neatness than fashion.

"Yes? Is there something you require?" she asked, eyebrows raised.

Her eyes really were quite remarkable, Edward thought.

"No. Yes. I mean to say, I am not accustomed to resting in the afternoon," he said.

"And you are bored, I suppose," she guessed. "Well, I am not at leisure to entertain you, cousin. I must finish these accounts for your father's inspection, and after that I must visit some of the tenants. This will be my last opportunity to do so before I leave for Brighton tomorrow."

"Might I accompany you on your visit to the tenants?"

Lydia looked surprised.

"My, you *are* desperate! If you wish to come, you are welcome. Be warned, though, that I shall make you carry the baskets."

"Fair enough," he said, glancing over her shoulder at the columns of neat figures. "Do you usually keep the accounts for the estate?"

"Yes," she said, continuing to write.

She closed the book after a moment and left it on the table. He noticed there were several others neatly bound together with cords at one side, ready for his father's inspection, he supposed.

Edward held her chair out for her as she rose, and she turned to face him. They were standing a bit too close, but she could not step back because the heavy table was behind her, and Edward did not choose to move. She smelled deliciously of lily of the valley scent, and her cheeks turned the delicate color of a ripe peach.

"When you do marry, you will be the master here unless your father dies before then," Lydia said, not quite looking at him. "When that time comes, I will be happy to explain anything in the ledgers that you do not understand."

"That is most generous of you, cousin," he said.

"Not at all. I offer this for the good of the estate and of its tenants. Not for you."

"I stand corrected," he said, trying not to smile.

"As long as we understand one another," she said briskly. "Shall we go?"

"See here, Cousin Lydia," Edward objected when he realized that Lydia was about to hook up the old but meticulously maintained gig to a job horse with her own two hands once they had loaded it with several heavy baskets. "That is no job for a lady. You had better let me do it."

"This lady has been doing the job for quite some time, but I thank you for your chivalrous offer just the same," she said.

"Do you seriously expect me to stand by while you harness that horse?"

"I am sorry if the prospect unmans you, but this horse kicked the last stranger who tried to get near her. She is old, but she still aims with deadly accuracy. If you wish, you may lead the horse out of the barn very carefully at arm's length by the bridle so no one will know that you did not hitch it to the gig yourself."

She was laughing at him, and Edward could not help laughing back.

"If I waited for an available man to do these things I would be waiting about forever," she explained, "and I am much too impatient for that, I fear. We had to let most of our male servants go years ago."

While she talked, she completed her task with quick, efficient movements. Then she straightened and looked at him expectantly. With a wry smile, he took the horse's bridle and led it outside.

"There now, my manly reputation is preserved," he said, noticing that she had donned a pair of leather gloves and had moved around to the driver's side of the gig. He almost offered to drive, but he found he had a strong desire to see his capable cousin handle the reins. Edward was highly amused by her look of utter astonishment when he took her hand in his and rested the other at the small of her back to assist her into the gig. Cousin Lydia obviously was not accustomed to these little courtesies. She charmed him by blushing a little.

"This is quite a handsome barn," he said, looking back at the structure over his shoulder.

"Thank you, Cousin Edward. It *should* be handsome," she said. "It took most of the profits from last year's harvest to pay for it. Vanessa sold a diamond necklace Alexander gave her to buy the milk cows and other livestock."

"That was a noble sacrifice on your sister's part," Edward said, feeling troubled.

"Yes, it was," she said, her smile fading. "I want you to remember that the next time your father starts accusing us of letting the place fall to rack and ruin."

"Cousin Lydia, I hope you know that I do not share my father's sentiments."

Her face softened.

"You were always the kindest of our cousins," she said. Then, as if embarrassed, she stared straight ahead. "Of course, that is not saying much. I think first we will visit Mr. Clancy, the bailiff, because I am certain you will have many questions to ask him. Then we will visit the tenants and deliver this food to those who need it."

"That sounds agreeable," he said, regretting that he had not paid attention when his father tried to interest him in estate matters.

By the time he had bowled along the country roads in the gig with Lydia and watched the tenants tip their hats to her, it became increasingly clear who actually ran this estate. The bailiff, while obviously a man of sense who knew the estate well, was elderly and not in the best health. His deference to Lydia's opinions was unmistakable.

"Mrs. Grundy!" she said, entering a tidy little cottage. "How do you feel today?"

"Not bad, Miss Lydia. Not bad," the old woman said. "How are my son and daughter-in-law?"

"As excellent a help as always," Lydia said, patting the old woman's hand. "Mrs. Grundy's son and daughter-in-law take care of us at the house," she added for Edward's benefit. "I do not know what we would have done without them. Mr. Whittaker, permit me to present Mrs. Grundy, one of our oldest tenants. Mrs. Grundy, Mr. Edward Whittaker, the new master of the estate."

"A pleasure, Mrs. Grundy," Edward said, distinctly getting the impression from the woman's shrewd expression that she already knew all about the circumstances surrounding the estate's change of ownership.

"Thank you, Mr. Whittaker," Mrs. Grundy said. She turned again to Lydia. "Are my son and daughter-in-law going with you to your new home, Miss Lydia, or will they return to the village?"

Lydia glanced at Edward.

"We will join my brother-in-law's household temporarily, so we will have no place for Mr. and Mrs. Grundy, I am afraid," she said. "I intend to discuss their situation with Mr. Whittaker before I leave."

"That is all right, then," the old lady said, apparently satisfied that Lydia would take care of her son's interests. Mrs. Grundy accepted a jar of soup and a round loaf of brown bread from Lydia with thanks after they had exchanged pleasantries about the weather.

The next few visits were not so enjoyable. Edward saw a young mother, who according to Lydia was due to deliver another child within days, perspiring in the stuffiness of an overcrowded cottage as her four other children watched Edward with big, frightened eyes. Lydia heated the soup on the fire and fed the children, all the while chatting cheerfully to the young mother. Rarely had Edward felt so useless, although by the end of the visit he somehow found a spoon in his hand and a child on his knee, dribbling Lydia's fragrant soup all over the both of them.

Then there was the young man whose leg had been amputated in the wars. This surly individual eyed Edward with dark suspicion the whole time Lydia and Edward made polite conversation with his parents.

"I was supposed to tell you that Mr. Clancy has work for you, and he wants you to report to him when your limb is healed enough for you to use the crutches," Lydia said casually to the young man as they were about to leave.

"If Mr. Clancy thinks I can be of use," the young man said with a shrug.

"Why should you not be of use?" Lydia asked, eyebrows raised. "You are young, and you still have two strong arms."

"Yes, Miss Lydia," the man said with surprising meekness. "I will talk to Mr. Clancy." When she gave him a straight look, he added, "I promise."

"There are so many of them," Edward said several hours later when he got back into the gig beside Lydia for the ride back to the house.

"I suppose your wife will do this when you marry," she said carefully, indicating the now empty baskets. "For now you can arrange with the curate's wife to look in on the sick and elderly for you." Her voice broke a little. "They deserve better than to be neglected, although heaven knows they did not fare as well as they should have while we were in charge."

"I shall see to it," he said, wanting to take the worried look off her face.

Her smile was like sunshine that had been hidden behind a cloud.

"Thank you, Cousin Edward," she said. "I know you will say it is none of my business how you deal with the tenants after we are gone, but I cannot stop thinking about them just because I am about to go to a new life."

"Yes. You are going to Brighton, are you not? What happens to you when the summer is over?"

Lydia gave him a surprised look.

"It is kind of you to ask, but you need not be concerned."

Edward looked at her sharply and saw that she was not being sarcastic. "My brother-in-law is making an unoccupied house on his estate available to us, and we will live with him and Vanessa until it is ready. Alexander is quite the most generous man in London, even if he is rather too insistent upon poking his nose into *my* affairs."

"Is he?" Edward asked, curious.

"Oh, yes. *I,* if you please, am to make my debut this spring in London."

"But are you not already out?" he asked. He supposed, since her older sister had made her come-out several years ago, that surely Lydia had been introduced to society by now.

"I go to parties in the neighborhood, of course, but I never expected to have a season in London. Before Vanessa married Alexander, I was quite resigned to the prospect of earning my own living as a governess or companion when Mother no longer needed me."

"How could you bear to be a mere dependent in a household of strangers?" Edward asked. He was shocked that she would consider such a thing.

"Quite easily, I promise you," she said. "The work could not be any harder than what I have been doing all along, and I would not have nearly so much responsibility."

"But have you no wish for a family and household of your own?"

"Of course, but one must be realistic," she said.

Edward looked at her aghast, and Lydia burst into laughter.

"Cousin Edward, do not look so gloomy. I shall do quite well, I promise you. We must hurry. Mrs. Grundy is preparing a nice beef roast and a ham, and she will be very put out if we are late."

"Are you always so worried about what your servants think?" he asked curiously.

"Certainly," Lydia said. "Mr. and Mrs. Grundy stayed to take care of us even when we could not pay their wages, so the least I owe them is a bit of consideration. They hope to stay on at the estate after we are gone, so I imagine she wishes to impress you with the excellence of her cooking."

"I see," Edward said. "Well, I am certainly hungry enough to do justice to Mrs. Grundy's dinner."

"If you and your father do not wish to retain her and her husband, send word to me and I will ask Alexander to provide them with the means to retire."

"It is not his responsibility, surely."

"No. But my mother has not the means, and I doubt that your father will have the inclination. Actually, I would vastly prefer that Alexander spend his money on a decent retirement for the Grundys than a splendid come-out for me."

Edward shook his head.

"Cousin Lydia, you are the most remarkable person."

"Not at all. You cannot know how much I dread making my bow to society at my advanced age. I shall be eighteen next year, older than most of the other debutantes. My mother is determined that I will do justice to the pretty gowns she means to tease Vanessa and Alexander into buying for me, so she is going to put me on a reducing diet of vinegar and soda biscuits. A delightful prospect, I assure you, for one who has always enjoyed a healthy country appetite."

"That is barbaric!" Edward exclaimed.

"I quite agree," Lydia said, "so you see that I would rather Alexander was not *quite* so helpful in arranging my life."

Edward gave a heavy sigh as he suddenly realized that he and Lydia were equally plagued with well-meaning relatives determined to dispose of their futures.

THREE

Lydia very correctly retired from the dining room table at the conclusion of the meal so the gentlemen could enjoy their port. Edward guessed she was glad to escape from his father's company.

"Not fit to drink," Henry said, scowling into his glass after taking a sip.

"Did you expect a household of females to lay in the best vintages?" Edward snapped, not bothering to conceal his exasperation with his father. "You certainly made it abundantly clear to Cousin Lydia that you consider her mother a spendthrift, so I should think this economy would meet with your approval."

Henry gave his son a sharp look.

"Your sense of chivalry does you credit, boy, but it is entirely misplaced. Annabelle Whittaker spent most of her income during the past several years living in high style in London and launching her oldest daughter upon society. She would be in Fleet Street Prison now if Blakely had not been so enamored of the chit that he paid her mother's debts."

"Yet the estate seems to be in remarkably good shape, and you can thank Cousin Lydia for that. It seems everyone from the lads who milk the cows to the bailiff is accustomed to taking orders from her."

Henry gave a harsh bark of laughter.

"That plain-faced, managing female?"

Edward stared at his father, amazed. Was he blind?

Lydia's hair was soft light brown, but it glimmered with subtle golden highlights from the sun. That same sun had tinted her fresh complexion to the healthy tan of a person who spent much time outdoors, but the result was to make her look vital rather than coarse. Her mouth was small and had a sensuous curve to the lower lip. Her nose could hardly be called petite, but it was straight, well shaped, and gave her face that indefinable quality known as "countenance."

When Cousin Lydia smiled with that mischievous twinkle in her eye, Edward could not help smiling along with her.

"I would not describe Cousin Lydia in quite that way," Edward said carefully. "Especially under her own roof."

"It is our roof now," Henry pointed out. "I wish Blakely luck in finding a husband for her. She probably will degenerate into a bossy spinster and spend the end of her days ruling his household unless he can foist her off onto some other unfortunate soul."

"I think she has behaved with unusual civility considering that we have come to evict her from her home."

"She hardly expresses herself with the deference one would expect toward those who have been her benefactors all these years," Mr. Whittaker said with a sniff of disdain.

"One can hardly blame her. You have made it abundantly clear that you do not feel obligated to treat her with common courtesy."

"Why should I? The connection does us no credit."

Disgusted, Edward announced his intention of joining Lydia in the parlor. But when he arrived, expecting to find his cousin engrossed in needlework or some other demure occupation, he found the room empty.

He heard a clatter and went into the hall to find Lydia struggling to drag a heavy trunk to the door.

"Let me help you," he said at once, relieving her of her burden.

"Thank you, Cousin Edward," she said, putting her hand to

the small of her back. "It is amazing how the accumulated mi-
nutiae of years will acquire so much bulk."

The trunk *was* heavy. He could not imagine how she had gotten
it down the stairs by herself.

"May I help you bring anything else?" he asked.

"No. That was the last of it. Would you like some tea, or do
you want to retire?"

"A cup of tea would be welcome, thank you," he said, although
he really just wanted to talk to her. Conversation with Lydia was
so stimulating. You never knew what she was going to say next.

Lydia rang for Mrs. Grundy, and the woman soon arrived with
tea and a plain but obviously fresh cake.

"That will be all for tonight, Mrs. Grundy," Lydia said. "I will
see to these things myself."

"Thank you, Miss Lydia," the woman said gratefully as she
left.

"Now, Cousin Edward," Lydia said as she poured the tea. "It
is time for you to satisfy my curiosity, since you probably learned
more than you wanted to know about my life this afternoon."

Edward smiled. "Certainly. What would you like to know?"

"How soon do you intend to marry? Do I know your future
wife?"

If another woman had asked, Edward might have taken the
comment as an indication of the lady's interest in him. But this
was Lydia, and he clearly heard the implied question.

Will she be a good mistress to my people?

"My parents are quite set on my marrying Lady Madelyn
Rathbone, although since I have not spoken to the lady I would
appreciate it if you would not tell anyone. It would be a trifle
premature, to say the least."

"I know Lady Madelyn," Lydia said. "Alexander's aunt, Lady
Letitia, is her godmother. She is very beautiful and accomplished."

This prim statement almost made Edward laugh. The expression on Lydia's face, though she tried to keep it neutral, made it plain that she did not care much for Lady Madelyn.

"Yes, she is," Edward said, deciding to leave it at that.

"And what are your plans?"

"Plans? I have none. I have spent the past few years in London sampling the delights of the metropolis, and I will continue to do so until my elders decide how I should dispose of my future."

"*That* is what you do with your time?" she said incredulously. "Drink and gamble?"

"Well, yes," he said, flinching a little under the censure in her eyes.

Whatever else she might have said was interrupted by a frantic knocking on the door.

Lydia jumped up and ran for the hallway with Edward at her heels.

"Mr. Edward," gasped his father's coachman. "The barn is on fire. We got your father's horses out, but—"

Lydia gave a cry of horror and ran outside. Edward caught up with her quickly.

"What are you doing?" he shouted. "Go back into the house."

"I certainly will *not!* The milk cows are in that barn!"

By that time Edward's father, swathed in his nightshirt, came running out into the yard.

"My horses!"

"They are safe," Edward said.

He grabbed Lydia by her shoulders and shoved her at his father.

"Take her back inside," Edward ordered as he ran for the barn.

"No!" shouted Lydia, struggling against her uncle's pinioning arms.

"This is no place for a female, you silly chit," Henry said in disgust. "You will just get in the way."

Lydia elbowed him in the stomach; when he grunted and released her, she followed Edward. She ran into the smoky barn and saw him and two footmen beating at the flames with blankets. When Edward looked up and saw her, he gave a cry of alarm.

"Lydia, get out!" he shouted. His heart leapt into his throat for fear that one of the huge, frightened cows might trample her.

"But the milk cows—"

"I will take them out myself if you will just go outside where it is safe." He started for the closest cow. *"Go,* Lydia," he shouted over his shoulder.

She picked up her skirts and ran.

The smoke was getting thick in the barn, and the frightened cows were mooing piteously and evading his efforts to free them, the perverse creatures! He got all four of them to the door and applied a swat to each ample backside to get them into the fresh air. His father's other footman came running with a bucket of water, followed by the coachman with another bucket. While the men applied themselves to the fire, Edward applied himself to getting Lydia's job horse out.

Fortunately the wind was not high, and so the flames were not spreading too fast.

When the animals were all outside, he noticed with approval that Lydia, Mr. and Mrs. Grundy, Edward's father, and the coachman had formed themselves into an efficient bucket brigade. The fire was little more than a half-hearted flame and a listless smudge pot when he went inside to help the coughing footmen.

To Edward's relief, Lydia did not return to the barn. He was thankful, and rather surprised, that she obeyed him.

When the fire was extinguished, he went outside to catch his breath. Then he looked across the yard and grinned.

Lydia was rounding up the cows. Even Edward's father was guiding one into a fenced portion of the yard. She should have looked silly, coaxing a cow along with her skirts flying, but she somehow managed to keep her dignity.

"They will be all right out here," Edward heard his father tell her when they walked back to him. He levered himself from the barn wall and went to meet them partway. "The barn door should be left open so the smoke will dissipate," Henry continued. "It may be difficult to convince the cows to go back inside the barn in the morning for milking if the smoke smell is still strong."

"If this does not cause their milk to dry up entirely," said Lydia worriedly. "I always keep the milk cows inside, but for one night—" She looked at Edward and her eyes widened.

"Cousin Edward!" she exclaimed, hurrying to him. "You have been hurt!"

"It is nothing."

"I will thank you not to tell me falsehoods, sir, for I can see very well that you have burned your arm from the way your coat is singed. And from the way you are limping it appears that you have done something to your leg as well. Come inside at once and let me have a look at you."

"My good girl, if you think I am about to strip off my pantaloons for your inspection, you can think again."

"I will have you know that I have spent most of my life patching up the men on this estate after one injury or another."

Lydia should have been blushing to the roots of her hair, but she only looked determined. Edward was afraid he was blushing.

"Well, you are not going to patch *me* up," he declared.

"Burns can be dangerous," she argued, putting her hands on her hips. Her soft brown hair had fallen halfway down her back and her eyes were snapping.

"You can look at my arm," he compromised, deciding that it would be no bad thing to let pretty Cousin Lydia smear something cool and soothing on his hurts.

"Very well," she said, satisfied. "Go to your room, and I will be there with my medical supplies directly."

"See here," said her uncle. "That would hardly be proper."

"You may come along, then, to make sure I will not take advantage of your precious son's innocence," Lydia said dryly. She started for the house, then turned back.

"Thank you for saving the barn," she said almost meekly. Looking a bit flustered, she turned abruptly and went to the house, leaving them to follow.

"Strange little thing," was Henry's only comment. "But I will say this for her—she does not lack for brains or a cool head."

"No," Edward agreed admiringly.

Henry gave his son a sharp look.

"She is still Annabelle Whittaker's daughter," he said. "And after today, she is no longer our concern."

Maybe not yours, Edward thought.

He is as beautiful as a god, thought Lydia as Edward sat before her on a straight chair in his bedroom wearing nothing but his flowing white shirt of fine cambric opened at the collar to reveal the strong column of his throat and skintight pantaloons. Lydia was not accustomed to seeing gentlemen in a state of undress, even though she had seen many of her laborers bare from the waist up and never thought a thing of it. Edward, whose broad shoulders, flat stomach, and sinewy limbs were revealed clearly beneath the thin fabric, was another matter entirely.

She rolled up the full sleeve of his shirt and began to wash the reddened, blistered skin of his arm carefully. She prayed she could touch him without trembling.

"It does not look so very bad," she said, uncomfortable with the silence between them. "I will give you some of this salve so you can apply it after I leave."

"Thank you, cousin," Edward said. "It is very soothing."

"Mrs. Grundy makes it from the herbs in her garden," Lydia said. "It is quite as good as anything one procures from a physician. Are you certain your leg does not need attention?"

"My leg is perfectly all right except for the bruise I shall probably have. Your horse kicked me. You were right about her. She does *not* like being handled by strangers."

Lydia forced herself to laugh even though she wanted to weep with relief that his injuries were not serious.

Edward was not a cruel man. He would not joke to others at her expense, telling them about the plump little cousin who acted like an idiot when they were alone together. But he would know the awful truth about her silly, fluttering heart unless she managed to keep her feelings in check, and she could not bear that.

Men like Edward—young, kind, handsome men with long pedigrees and the expectation of inheriting a fortune—were not for Lydia. Not when they were in a fair way to becoming engaged to beautiful, rich, accomplished young women like Lady Madelyn Rathbone.

Lydia decided it was a very good thing she was leaving tomorrow. Too much of Cousin Edward's company would only make her discontented with her lot in life.

"There. I think you will do," she said briskly.

To her surprise, Edward caught her hand and, keeping his eyes on hers, he kissed it.

"You are a remarkable person, Cousin Lydia," he said.

He does not mean to be cruel, Lydia told herself. *He means it as a kindness to his poor country cousin.*

She forced a smile to her lips.

"Nonsense," she said as she hastily withdrew her hand and finished gathering the basin and cloths. When she had everything, she walked to the door, being careful not to splash any of the water in the basin onto the floor. Her hands were not quite steady.

Stop acting like a schoolgirl, she chided herself in disgust.

"Cousin Lydia."

She turned but could not quite look at him.

"I am more sorry than I can say for the way my family has treated yours."

"It was not of your doing."

"If there is anything I can do—"

"There is nothing," she said firmly, and left the room.

Alexander pulled up in front of the house with the traveling coach very early the next morning. He had decided to come in person to fetch Lydia, determined to deal with her uncle despite her assurances that she did not need his support. It disturbed him that he almost had fallen into the comfortable habit, as had Lydia's mother and sisters, of letting Lydia deal alone with any unpleasant family business.

That would come to an end immediately. When Henry Whittaker arrived, Alexander would make it abundantly clear that he had distressed his sister-in-law and her daughters for the last time.

Lydia herself came to the door. The trunk with her worldly possessions in it resided in the hall awaiting removal.

"Alexander," she said, looking relieved to see him. "I had not expected you so early!"

"I wanted to arrive before your uncle," he said, taking his coat off and putting it on his arm.

"Then I am afraid you are too late. He arrived yesterday," she said wryly.

"Poor Lydia," he exclaimed. "What possessed the man to come a day earlier than expected?"

"I have no idea," she said, grasping the handle of the heavy trunk. She was obviously in a hurry to be gone.

"Do not bother with that," he told her. "My servants will carry it out to the coach. How awkward this is! It never occurred to me that you would be forced to shelter your uncle overnight with only the Grundys to lend you respectability."

Lydia laughed.

"It was even worse than that. My uncle brought along my cousin Edward. I have spent the night here with not one gentleman, but *two.*"

Alexander was properly taken aback.

"Do you think my reputation can ever be recovered after this?" Lydia said, putting her hand to her brow in a dramatic gesture.

Her brother-in-law rolled his eyes.

"I am glad you can laugh. The two of them must have given you the devil's own time."

"Uncle Henry has been disagreeable, but I expected that. However, despite the awkwardness, I am rather glad Cousin Edward came along. A fire broke out in the barn and he and his father's servants managed to rescue the cows and put the fire out before too much damage was done."

"Is that why the cows are all standing in the yard?"

"The cows! Oh, Good Lord! They must have gotten outside the fence!"

She would have run outside to gather the cows herself if Alexander had not caught her arm.

"Lydia! This place is no longer your responsibility," he said. "Let your uncle deal with the bloody cows!"

Lydia put her hands on her hips and stuck her jaw out.

"Those *bloody* cows were paid for by—"

"I know, I know," Alexander said, flinching at her repetition of his improper language. "The bloody diamond necklace. Do you not think I would have found a way to discover who bought it and get it back if I thought Vanessa regretted losing it? I bought her a better one on our honeymoon."

"Cousin Lydia."

Both of them looked up to see Edward standing at the entrance to the hall, regarding them curiously.

"Cousin Edward," Lydia said. "Alexander, this is—"

"Mr. Whittaker," Alexander interrupted. "I trust you and your father found all satisfactory." His voice dared him to say otherwise.

"Lord Blakely," said Edward. "Yes, I thank you. Cousin Lydia has been taking splendid care of us."

The gentlemen bowed solemnly. Lydia noticed they did not take their eyes off one another.

Men, she thought with disgust.

"Do not worry about the cows," Edward said cheerfully. Lydia wondered how long he had been listening to their conversation. "I shall find my father's servants and we shall round them up directly."

This last was directed to Lydia with a warm smile as he passed her to go out the front door.

Alexander gave Lydia a straight look.

"He behaved himself, I trust?"

"You are beginning to sound exactly like Mother," Lydia said, rolling her eyes. "Cousin Edward was the soul of propriety. I was perfectly safe, I assure you, except from my uncle's ill-natured remarks. Since my own behavior was hardly conciliating, however, you need not worry overmuch about my sensibilities."

"Then, let us get the business over with," Alexander said. "The sooner we are back in Brighton, the better."

Alexander's meeting with Lydia's uncle was brief and to the point.

"I have here all of the legal documents pertaining to the estate, the livestock, the tenant agreements, in short, everything of Mrs. Whittaker's that you need to carry on the business of the estate," he said, indicating the paperwork that Lydia had left in organized piles on the library table. "Understand that by handing over the estate to you, Mrs. Whittaker and her daughters now consider their relationship with you at an end. Any further communication between you and Mrs. Whittaker will be initiated with me through my solicitor in London. Are we agreed?"

This statement conveyed Alexander's contempt for Uncle Henry so effectively that the elder man's face reddened with suppressed fury.

"Yes. Very well," he said, accepting the documents.

"That concludes our business, I believe," Alexander said with a wintry smile. He turned to Lydia and offered his arm. "Are you ready, my dear?"

"Yes, Alexander," she said.

She already had said her farewells to Mr. and Mrs. Grundy. Her trunk had been loaded into the coach by Alexander's servants.

She was going, she thought with a thrill of panic. She really was going.

Lydia took Alexander's arm and walked out the front door of her home, knowing that she would never see it again. The house looked beautiful in the early morning sunlight.

Once inside the coach, she leaned her head back against the squabs and closed her eyes.

"Lydia?"

She opened her eyes. Alexander was looking at her anxiously.

"Do not worry about me, Alexander. I am not particularly sentimental, you know," she lied.

"Who the devil is that?" Alexander asked irritably.

Lydia looked in the direction of his nod and saw a rider was keeping pace with the coach. Lydia realized the rider was Edward, and he was signaling for the vehicle to stop.

"Oh, very well," said Alexander impatiently, giving the appropriate order.

Alexander peered out of the coach at Edward when the footman opened the door.

"What do you want?" he demanded.

Edward dismounted and took off his hat.

"A word with Cousin Lydia alone, if I may."

"Certainly not," Alexander snapped.

Lydia poked at Alexander's back and gestured for him to let down the steps. Scowling, he obeyed.

Edward's touch sent a pleasant warmth right through Lydia's glove when he took her hand and assisted her in stepping down from the coach.

Stop that, she told herself firmly.

Edward took her arm and led her a little distance away.

"That is far enough," Alexander shouted, getting out of the coach and standing to face them with his arms folded across his broad chest.

"Very well," Edward said. He turned to Lydia. "Cousin, I wanted to assure you that I talked to my father last night, and he has agreed to keep the Grundys on for the time being. I also will speak to the pastor's wife about the tenants' needs, and I will make sure the expense for seeing to them comes from us and not from her own pocket."

"You are very kind, Cousin Edward," Lydia said warmly. "Thank you for setting my mind at rest."

"Take care of yourself," he said solemnly.

"I will. I hope you will be happy in your new home," she replied.

"Thank you." Edward glanced at Alexander and gave Lydia a mischievous smile. "He looks dreadfully cross," he added softly. Alexander's eyes narrowed and he took a step closer to them. "What does he think I am going to do? Ravish you right here on the open road?"

"Alexander thinks I need a man's protection," she said primly.

"He does not know you very well, then, does he?" Edward said. He tucked her arm in his and escorted her back to the coach. Then he bowed and kissed her hand. His smile when he straightened told Lydia that this gallant performance was for Alexander's benefit.

Edward mounted his horse and raised his hat in salute so his fair hair glistened in the sun.

"Puppy," Alexander said with a scowl, exactly as if he were fifty years old instead of less than thirty. "Well, I am glad that business is finished. You can be comfortable again, my dear, for you never have to see that fellow again."

"No, indeed," Lydia said glumly.

FOUR

Brighton
July, 1814

Her mother and sisters were delighted to see her, but it was plain that Lydia no longer held her old position of responsibility in their family circle. She had expected to find them at sixes and sevens, waiting eagerly for her to arrive and set them all to rights.

Instead, she found that Alexander's capable servants and the hotel staff saw to all her family's needs perfectly well without the slightest assistance from Annabelle Whittaker's bossy second daughter.

She felt utterly deflated and at a loss how to occupy her time for the first time in years.

Lydia's cheese-paring ways that had ensured her fatherless family's survival through their darkest periods were now gaily mocked. Even her little sisters joined in the game of playfully wagging their fingers at Lydia and telling her not to be such a miser when she suggested what she considered to be reasonable economies.

Her mother trilled with laughter when Lydia suggested that they order a plain dinner of chicken from the hotel kitchens on an evening when they were not expecting company.

"You have plagued us with your old chicken dinners for the last time, missy," she said gaily.

Her mother had not meant to be cruel. Lydia knew this. But she resented being treated like a simpleton just because she did not think it right for them to be extravagant with Alexander's money. When Lydia found out how much her mother was spending on lavish dinners and clothes for herself and the girls, she felt ready to sink.

Alexander, however, considered Lydia's attempts to introduce a spirit of economy into her mother's living arrangements to be as unnecessary as her mother and sisters did. He told her so when she suggested that perhaps she, her mother, and sisters should move to a less expensive hotel.

"Your concern for my purse is touching, my dear," he said with maddening condescension, "but before I married Vanessa I used to spend more in a single night at the tables than I have spent these several weeks on your family's needs. After their years of deprivation, they deserve to enjoy themselves a little."

Years of deprivation? He was talking about the existence that Lydia had worked so hard to provide for them. Apparently none of them appreciated her efforts. On the contrary, they behaved as if she had deliberately deprived them of all the little luxuries that they could ill afford.

But what could she say to Alexander? A son of Annabelle's own body could not have been more generous or considerate toward her and her daughters. Lydia swallowed her resentment and tried not to be ungrateful.

"Darling, this is Brighton. The Prince Regent's own city," Mrs. Whittaker said with a frown when Lydia insisted that she did not need new clothes for the summer. In Lydia's opinion, her old gowns were perfectly adequate for sightseeing, shepherding her little sisters on walks in the park, and receiving calls from her mother's acquaintances. Soon they would leave Brighton to move into Alexander's country home, and who would see her new clothes in the country?

More laughter and wagging fingers. Who would see her in the country? Why, *everyone!* As relatives by marriage of the Earl of Stoneham and his heir, the Whittakers would dine with all the important families in the neighborhood.

Vanessa unexpectedly accosted Lydia one morning, insisted that she exchange her morning dress for street clothes, and bundled her into her carriage as Lydia's mother and sisters watched from the window. Lydia could see from their smug smiles that they had plotted against her, and it was an effort not to feel betrayed.

"Alexander will be very hurt, my dear, if you refuse his gift of a few new dresses," Vanessa said, brushing Lydia's objections aside.

"Unless you tell him, I doubt that he will know the difference," Lydia grumbled. "One gown looks much like another to a man."

Vanessa rolled her eyes.

"He would know," she said dryly. "It may seem unkind for me to say so, but your appearance does us no credit, my dear."

"What is wrong with my appearance?" Lydia demanded.

"You are dressed with neatness and propriety, which is all very well when one is living quite out of the world. But I will have you know, my dear, we move in quite smart circles now," she said. "Alexander's military friends and, of course, connections of his father's frequently call on us. Think of Alexander. He will take his seat in Parliament next year."

"I doubt that his credibility will be damaged beyond repair if his sister-in-law is seen in public wearing an outmoded gown," Lydia said dryly.

"Lydia, no one appreciates the sacrifices you have made for this family more than I do, but our circumstances have changed. Do you not understand?"

"I understand perfectly." Lydia's jaw clenched. "Now that I am no longer needed to keep the household accounts, supervise the girls, and contrive a way to keep us from starving, I am an embarrassment to my family."

"Lydia, *no!*" cried Vanessa, horrified. "How can you say such a thing?"

"Because it is true. You have been treating me like a simple-minded idiot since I came to Brighton."

"I have done no such thing!"

"Oh? Then stop looking down your nose and calling me 'my dear' in that odiously superior tone every time you take breath. You are beginning to sound just like Lady Letitia."

Since Lady Letitia, Alexander's fashionable aunt, was quite the greatest snob of their acquaintance, Vanessa could not be expected to accept this accusation with composure.

The ladies proceeded to Vanessa's chosen dressmaker's establishment in uncomfortable silence. Once there, Vanessa and the dressmaker bent over pattern cards and illustrations in *La Belle Assemblee* as they had an earnest discussion about what would become Lydia best. Listlessly, Lydia looked at fabric, reflecting that once she would truly have enjoyed the prospect of new clothes not of her own making. But after so many years of scrimping and purse-pinching, she found she could not make up her mind. Her choices had always been dictated by what fabrics were cheapest—which meant settling for colors that were not those in fashion. Lydia did not even know which colors were in fashion.

In the end, Vanessa and the dressmaker made her choices for her, and Lydia was promised delivery of the gowns by the end of the week.

"Thank you, Vanessa," Lydia said stiffly once they were back in the carriage. "I am sure I will enjoy wearing them."

"You are most welcome, my—Lydia," Vanessa said, looking uncharacteristically subdued.

Lydia felt tears start to her eyes.

Vanessa always had been her ally and confidante in the Her-culean effort to keep their mother from outrunning the constable. Now, it seemed, Vanessa had new loyalties and many fashionable new acquaintances whose good opinion mattered more to her than her sister's feelings.

In addition to losing her home, it seemed that Lydia had lost her best friend.

One of the Whittaker ladies' many visitors in Brighton was Mrs. Coomb, Mrs. Whittaker's cousin. This lady had married well and was determined to cut a dash in society for the benefit of her dainty, blond fifteen-year-old daughter, Amelia, who, like Lydia, was to be presented at court the following spring.

Violetta Coomb, a plump, pretty widow who bore a striking resemblance to her cousin Annabelle, had managed to keep her distance during the Whittakers' years of poverty. But now that Mrs. Whittaker had succeeded in marrying her eldest daughter to the heir to an earldom, Mrs. Coomb was eager to renew her acquaintance with her cousin and foster a friendship between their daughters.

"It is such a pity that you will be leaving for the country tomorrow when I have just found you again, my dear cousin," Mrs. Coomb lamented.

"We shall all meet again in London for the Season," Mrs. Whittaker reminded her cheerfully.

"How happy Amelia will be to see her dear friend Lydia again," Mrs. Coomb went on.

If Amelia was surprised to learn that Lydia, with whom she had not exchanged a dozen words, was her dear friend, she had the tact not to show it.

"Yes, indeed," Amelia said, smiling at Lydia.

"But Annabelle! I have just had the most brilliant idea! Why do you not leave Lydia behind to stay in Brighton a week or two as our guest? Amelia will enjoy her company, for she is always wanting to be on the go, and she quite exhausts me."

Lydia smiled cynically at Amelia's look of dismay. The girl

might well look horrified at having a full-time watchdog set upon her. Not for a minute did Lydia think that Mrs. Coomb had any other object in mind apart from the obvious one of ingratiating herself with cousins who had moved up in the world. Amelia's beauty and flirtatious ways had attracted the attention of a certain handsome officer of the 10th Hussars, the Prince Regent's own regiment, which was stationed at Brighton. Lydia knew that Mrs. Coomb had been at her wits' end to foil the elaborate stratagems Amelia and her admirer employed to meet in secret.

Obviously Mrs. Coomb instantly identified Lydia as a strait-laced person who had the energy to play gooseberry for her precocious daughter.

"What a delightful scheme!" Annabelle exclaimed. "Lydia has had no opportunity to meet girls her own age out in the country. I am certain she would enjoy a visit in Brighton with such a delightful companion as dear Amelia."

"Mother, surely I will be wanted in the country to help you settle into the house," Lydia objected.

Mrs. Whittaker gave the annoying trill of laughter that indicated Lydia was being silly again.

"Certainly not! We have servants for such things," she said grandly.

Her message could not have been more clear. Lydia was neither wanted nor needed by her family. They would do very well without her.

Lydia swallowed the lump in her throat. She had no choice but to give in.

Within minutes the matter was settled, and Amelia and Lydia regarded one another with trepidation.

"Trifling with schoolgirls is an excellent way to end up having grass before breakfast with some irate father or elder brother, my lad," Edward Whittaker warned his fellow officer,

Lieutenant Quentin Lowell of the Prince of Wales's Own Royal 10th Hussars, when the man waxed poetical about the charms of Miss Amelia Coomb, a young lady barely out of the school-room, and about the couple's attempts to be private with one another.

Edward had no sooner moved his personal effects into the barracks and donned his new uniform when the lovesick Lieu-tenant Lowell enlisted his aid in separating his young lady from the dragon who had been set to chaperon the couple.

"Amelia has no father or brother," the besotted Lowell pointed out. "Just a slightly dotty mother. All you have to do is draw the cousin off so Amelia and I can have a decent con-versation without her listening to every word. The cousin might even be a relative of yours. Miss Lydia Whittaker. Do you know her?"

Edward's head shot up.

"I have a cousin by that name, yes."

"Brown hair, blue eyes, a bit plump and quiet."

"It sounds like Cousin Lydia except for the quiet part," Ed-ward said, smiling reminiscently. "The lady I know has plenty to say, and she is not at all shy about expressing her opinion. I would be pleased to see her again."

"Capital!" exclaimed Quentin, clapping Edward on the shoulder.

Lydia gave a long-suffering sigh as she watched Lieutenant Lowell rush immediately to Amelia's side with the barest show of courtesy toward Mrs. Coomb. Lydia could see another boring afternoon ahead, walking with the couple along the seashore to maintain the illusion of propriety for the benefit of passersby.

She always felt like a fool on such occasions. Lieutenant Lowell, while perfectly polite, clearly did not want Lydia along. But the hungry look in his eyes whenever he looked at Amelia made it plain to even so easygoing a lady as Mrs. Coomb that it would be the height of folly to leave the two alone together.

Lydia quite saw Mrs. Coomb's dilemma. Lieutenant Lowell would be a respectable match for Amelia once she grew up a little. But at fifteen, Amelia was too young for marriage. More-over, Mrs. Coomb did not want to promise her daughter to a suitor before her debut in London next spring. In London, so beautiful a girl might attract the notice of a viscount or even an earl. But there was also the chance she might not, so Mrs. Coomb was reluctant to discourage Lieutenant Lowell's atten-tions altogether.

Lydia glanced at the couple to make sure Lieutenant Lowell was not being too particular in his attentions to Amelia, since Mrs. Coomb was occupied in greeting his companion, another member of the 10th Hussars. She could see the shoulder of his blue uniform coat and a bit of gold lacing, although little else of the gentleman was visible because another visitor's enormous hat hid his face from her.

"Miss Whittaker," Lieutenant Lowell said, looking up from his rapt contemplation of Amelia's exquisite countenance. "I took the liberty of bringing along a gentleman I fancy is not unknown to you."

By that time his companion had come into the room.

Lydia was utterly speechless, for standing before her was Edward. With laughter in his eyes at her astonishment, he bowed to her. Recollecting herself, she bowed back.

Slowly she walked all the way around him, taking in the meticulously tailored uniform of the 10th Hussars. He carried a tall black fur hat with a plume, and he wore gleaming Hessian boots. Her eyes fastened on his face.

"A mustache?" she asked quizzically.

"Very *good,* cousin," he said, his laughing silver eyes sof-tening the sarcasm. "I knew I could depend on so clever a lady to recognize it at once. It seems our colonel, the Prince Regent, thinks a mustache is an indispensable component of the Hussar image, so we are ordered to grow them."

Lydia touched her cousin's upper lip with a gentle forefinger. It was quite a nice mustache, actually. It made him look dashing and a bit dangerous.

"Why did you not tell me?" she asked. "You let me believe you had no purpose in life save that of dissipation."

"It was by no means a settled thing when we last spoke. Did you not disapprove of my idleness and imply that my life needed some useful direction?"

"I did not mean something that could get you *killed!*" she snapped.

Surprise flickered over his face, and Lydia was embarrassed. She sounded as if she had a right to care what happened to him, which she certainly did not.

"Highly unlikely, cousin," he said wryly. "Now that the country is at peace, I am in no danger of being damaged unless I fall off my horse during a parade. My parents would hardly risk my precious skin by permitting me to join an active regiment while there is the least danger of combat."

He sounded bitter, and Lydia recalled that as a youth Edward had been army mad.

"Ladies, would you like to accompany us on a walk by the seaside?" Lieutenant Lowell interjected. "It is a fine day."

"I should like it of all things," said Amelia, looking up adoringly into her admirer's face.

"Mrs. Coomb?" Lydia said, looking to her hostess for permission.

"Certainly, my dears. Run along and have a good time," that lady said benevolently. "And take your pelisse, Amelia. We cannot have you coming down with a chill."

"Yes, Mama," Amelia said, still smiling into Lieutenant Lowell's besotted face.

* * *

"My cousin is an innocent girl, and I will not have her trifled with," Lydia said sternly when Edward deliberately slowed his steps to give the other couple more privacy.

"They are only *talking,* Lydia," he said reasonably. "They can hardly do anything else in such a public place."

"He is a hardened rake, if rumor is to be believed. I expect you to help me keep Amelia safe from his attentions."

"I?" Edward exclaimed, taken aback. "I hesitate to disappoint you, but I am considered to be a bit of a rake myself. It would be like putting the wolf in charge of the hen house to expect me to guard the fair Amelia's virtue, I promise you."

"Oh, *really,*" Lydia scoffed, highly amused. "Anyone can see you are not nearly so bad as he is."

"Indeed?" Edward asked as an imp of mischief took possession of his mind. He stopped their progress and drew Lydia toward him, then tilted her chin up with his fingers. Her skin was so soft, and her sensual lips formed a small "o" of surprise. *Lilies of the valley,* he thought, enjoying the scent of her skin. Sweet. Virginal.

So innocent.

Lydia looked delightful today in an attractive walking costume of primrose colored dress, ivory pelisse, and a matching primrose straw hat trimmed with ivory flowers and streamers that fluttered in the breeze. He was pleased to see her dressed more in keeping with her station. Lydia did not seem to have the least idea of how appealing she was, which added immeasurably to her charm.

"When did a little girl like you become such an authority on the subject of rakes?" he whispered.

Her eyes grew wide and she gave a startled gasp when Edward cupped her soft cheek in his hand and stopped a hairsbreadth away from touching his lips to hers. Her consternation was so adorable that he could not help smiling.

Incredibly, she smiled right back.

"Was this supposed to frighten me?" she asked, assuming a tone of bravado.

Edward could tell by her flushed face that Lydia was by no means as impervious to his touch as she pretended, so it was with some regret that he allowed her to save face.

"I suppose it was," he admitted, dropping his hand and stepping back. "Very well, my dear. Rest assured that I shall do my best to keep Lowell in check."

"Just remember, Cousin Edward," she said, mollified, "that although Amelia is a softhearted girl who is willing to trust anyone, I intend to protect her from being imposed upon by Lieutenant Lowell."

"Yes, *ma'am*," Edward said, keeping his tone light. He wondered if Lydia had any idea how much she almost had needed someone to protect her from him.

FIVE

Amelia begged and begged, so finally her softhearted mother gave in, even though Amelia was not precisely out and it was not quite the thing for her to appear at a ball given at the Castle Inn.

It was true, Mrs. Coomb admitted, that August in Brighton was becoming thin of company as the fashionable world left for London and the little season, so no one of any consequence was likely to witness this small impropriety.

"Quentin!" Amelia cried when Lieutenant Lowell and Lieutenant Whittaker called the next day. "Mama has agreed! I can go to the ball."

In her excitement she threw herself into his arms, forgetting completely that proper young ladies did not call their beaus by their first names until they were in a fair way of being betrothed, and that it was not at *all* the thing for a young lady to embrace a young man not related to her with such enthusiasm.

"Amelia!" exclaimed the young lady's mother, quite scandalized. Amelia's pretty face flushed scarlet, and Lieutenant Lowell stepped back from her with a self-conscious laugh.

"That is capital news, Miss Coomb," Lieutenant Lowell said, clearly as delighted as Amelia. "You must put me down for the first two dances."

Lydia had stared in surprise that Amelia would commit such an indiscretion in front of her mother, herself, and two visitors.

But Amelia was very young, after all, and even after such short acquaintance, it was apparent to Lydia that when Amelia gave her heart, she gave it completely.

"Cousin Lydia," Edward said, catching her arm and giving her a little shake. Lydia blinked and looked at him, aware that he had addressed a remark to her.

"I beg your pardon. I was not attending."

"You have an uncommon skill for wounding a man's vanity," he said wryly. "I was asking you to put me down for the first two dances at the ball."

"I shall not be going," Lydia said, taken aback.

"Of course you will. Who is going to make certain that Quentin will not spirit Miss Coomb away to Gretna Green at midnight?" he said, lowering his voice.

"Her mother, I imagine," Lydia said dryly. "In any event, my attending a ball is out of the question. I do not even own a decent ball gown."

Having an unerring ear for talk of fashion, Amelia overheard this last remark.

"Lydia, you can wear one of my ball gowns," Amelia offered. "I have two, for we just had them made up in London before we came to Brighton."

"I thank you for your offer, but I shall split the seams right out of any gown of yours," Lydia said, giving Amelia's slim figure a quizzical look from head to foot. She had not missed Mrs. Coomb's look of dismay. That lady was naturally reluctant to see one of Amelia's gowns damaged by the struggles of her plump cousin to wriggle into it.

"You can wear one of mine, then," Mrs. Coomb, a lady built on more queenly lines, said to Lydia in a relieved tone. "I have brought several."

"There! It is settled," said Edward. "Your first two dances are mine, if you please, Cousin Lydia. And, Miss Coomb, I hope you will honor me with your second two."

"I should be delighted, Lieutenant Whittaker," Amelia said, blushing prettily.

It was her first ball, and Amelia could talk of nothing else. For the first time since Lydia came to Brighton, Amelia declined Lieutenant Lowell's suggestion of a walk along Marine Parade.

"We have so much to do before the ball," she said, looking up at Lieutenant Lowell through her eyelashes. "I hope you will excuse us."

"Of course," that gentleman said, taking the hint and rising to take leave of their hostess. Edward stood as well.

"You are displeased with me," Edward whispered to Lydia under cover of the general conversation.

She stared at him in surprise. How had he known?

"I did not want to go to the ball," she whispered back, "and you have made it impossible for me to escape from it."

"Then I will not offer you an apology because I am not in the least repentant," he said with a smile. "I should not enjoy it half so much without your company."

Lydia gave a snort of laughter. "At any rate, your punishment will be terrible, I promise you, for I shall be stepping all over your feet. I am a woefully incompetent dancer."

"I do not believe that," Edward said with a smile.

"You shall see," she said, trying to look ominous. "Be sure to wear your heaviest boots to the ball."

As soon as the gentlemen were gone Amelia insisted upon going through her mother's clothes to find a ball gown for Lydia.

"Mama's new pink lace gown would become you, Lydia," she said excitedly, startling her mother's maid by brushing past her and yanking open the door of the wardrobe.

"Absolutely not, Amelia," Lydia said, sympathizing with Mrs. Coomb's look of dismay. "I would not dream of wearing your mother's new gown before she has had a chance to wear it herself."

Mrs. Coomb let out the breath she had been holding.

"I had not thought," Amelia said. "And it would have to be taken in all over because Mama is larger than you are."

Tactless though this remark was, it made Mrs. Coomb look much more cheerful.

"Too true, darling," she said with a twinkle. "I fear I have indulged myself far too much among the excellent pastries to be had here. I have a number of gowns in my wardrobe that are too small for me and would fit Lydia admirably with only the slightest alteration. Normally I give all of my gowns to my maid when I am finished with them, but since she usually sells them anyway, altering one of the gowns so you can wear it for one night should not matter to her in the slightest."

She turned to her maid, who had been standing by, eyes wide with horror at the mess the enthusiastic Amelia was making among Mrs. Coomb's clothes.

"You will not mind, will you, Sanders?"

"Not at all, mum," the maid said, already scanning Lydia's figure with the eye of an accomplished needlewoman. "I can think of several things that might do, if I might show you."

"Very well, Sanders," Mrs. Coomb said in relief.

Lydia was relieved, too. She could safely be guided by Mrs. Coomb's maid without fear that she would choose something her mistress would rather not have altered.

"This one," the maid said, drawing out a pretty gown in periwinkle blue. "And it is hardly worn, mum, because we agreed the color did not become you even before it became a bit too tight. It would look very well on Miss Whittaker."

"Yes, Lydia," Amelia said, taking the gown and holding it up to Lydia's face so she could show Lydia the effect in the cheval glass. "It is exactly the color of your eyes."

Lydia had to agree that the color was lovely. The style was a bit matronly, but it would do well enough.

The afternoon before the ball, Lydia dressed Amelia's lustrous blond hair in a complicated arrangement of gathered curls at the crown as Lydia had so often dressed Vanessa's before she was married. Lydia had a knack for hairdressing, and she often told her sisters that if their situation got too dire she could always find herself a job as a superior lady's maid by cultivating a false French accent and walking about with her nose in the air.

"How well that looks, Lydia," said Mrs. Coomb when she came into her daughter's room to inspect the result.

"I look so much older!" Amelia said, pleased.

"There will come a time, my child," said Mrs. Coomb indulgently, "when you will not consider that such a good thing."

Amelia made a wry face and turned to Lydia.

"It is your turn now, Lydia. How are we going to arrange your hair?"

"I thought I would draw it up at the crown and allow some curls to fall over the shoulder. Too many curls around my face only makes it look fatter."

"Lydia," Amelia said sternly. "Your face is not fat."

"Dear heart, my cheekbones disappeared sometime during my childhood and they have yet to emerge. Plump. Let us say plump instead of fat, by all means. It means the same thing, but it sounds ever so much kinder."

"You would be quite pretty if you would fix yourself up a little," Amelia insisted. "I notice that Lieutenant Whittaker has been quite attentive these past few weeks."

"Such an innocent," Lydia said wryly. "I strongly suspect Cousin Edward has been bribed handsomely by your young man to keep me at a distance so Lieutenant Lowell can whisper sweet compliments in your ear without my spoiling sport."

"Is that why he asked you for the first two dances?" Amelia tried to look arch, but the effect was so comical on her young face that Lydia could only laugh.

By the time the ladies were enthroned in all their finery in Mrs. Coomb's carriage, Lydia was surprised to find herself nervous about the ball. *Nonsense,* she told herself in disgust. *You are no romantic schoolgirl to expect anything wonderful to happen at your first ball.* She knew very well her silly heart was doing flip-flops because she was promised to Cousin Edward for the first set.

When she walked into the ballroom at the Castle Inn with Mrs. Coomb and Amelia, though, the first gentleman to accost her was not Cousin Edward, but her neighbor from Yorkshire, Robert Langtry.

"Lydia, old thing!" he said heartily, looking pleased to see her. "You are looking well."

"Thank you, Robert," she said, "or Mr. Langtry, I *should* say."

"Lord, Lydia. Do not go all missish on me, I beg. We have known one another since the cradle and we can hardly be expected to stand on ceremony with one another now. Come along. The first set is forming."

He seized her hand before she could say another word. She was about to explain that the dance was taken when Edward appeared at her side and gave Robert a look that should have frozen him as solid as the Thames in January.

"I believe," he said, "that Miss Whittaker is promised to me for the first two dances."

Lydia could only stare. Who was this intimidating military gentleman? This was the first time she had seen Edward in his dress uniform, and it was enough to make her knees go weak. Was this the cheerful man who had joked with her over the past few weeks? He looked positively dangerous.

Robert, on the other hand, merely looked bewildered.

How ridiculous, Lydia thought, barely repressing the impulse to roll her eyes. Of course, Robert should have *asked* her if she was engaged for the dance, but it probably never occurred to him that she would be. At informal parties in Yorkshire, Robert often had taken pity on Lydia as she sat with the other wallflowers.

"Cousin Edward, this is our neighbor—your neighbor now, actually—Mr. Robert Langtry. Mr. Langtry, Lieutenant Whittaker of the Royal 10th Hussars, my father's nephew."

"You mean he's the son of horrid—er, I mean your Uncle Henry?" Robert blurted out in surprise. Lydia knew he had often listened to Mrs. Whittaker's avowals of eternal enmity against Uncle Henry, his children and his children's children. Robert's amiable face grew stern. "Your solicitude for the members of your uncle's fatherless family certainly does you credit, Lieutenant Whittaker," he added dryly.

Edward looked as if he might like to respond to this deliberate provocation, but he obeyed the command implicit in the sharp elbow Lydia jabbed at his ribs. Instead, he favored Robert with a slight bow. Robert returned it.

"If you will excuse us," Edward said coldly.

"Certainly," Robert said, showing all his teeth. Edward turned to escort to Lydia to the dance floor. "Lydia," Robert added, "if you are not promised for the second set, I should like to dance with you."

Lydia could feel Edward's back stiffen.

"It is promised as well, Robert," Lydia called over her shoulder as Edward inexorably led her away. "But I shall be happy to give you the third set."

She gave Edward's arm a yank.

"Cousin Edward, whatever is the matter with you?" she exclaimed. "I shall be completely out of breath just by *running* to the dance floor and have none left for the dance itself."

"My apologies," he said, slowing his steps. "I see Quentin and Miss Coomb are forming a set and I thought it would be pleasant for us to join it, but we must be quick or another couple will arrive there first."

"That is not what I mean, and you know it," she said sternly. "Really, Cousin Edward, you were looking at him as if some rival dog had tried to snatch a bone away from you. I have rarely felt so ridiculous in my life."

"You used his first name," Edward said.

"Well, I have been using it since I was in short skirts, so it is hard to keep remembering to call him Mr. Langtry now that we are grown up."

"Still, the fellow seems awfully familiar in his manner toward you."

"We pledged to marry when we were children," Lydia said wryly. "But then Vanessa grew up to be so beautiful that I was soon forgotten, alas."

They had arrived at the set and joined hands across from Lieutenant Lowell and an ebullient Amelia.

They started forward to bow to the opposite couple, then bowed to each other. Edward favored her with one of his dazzling smiles, and she almost missed a step.

Lydia told herself, *firmly,* that Edward's beauty was merely a random act of Providence, and he could not help the unfortunate effect his smile had on susceptible females, of which Lydia was *not* one.

"You were hoaxing me," he said after a few moments. She had no idea what he meant. "You dance quite well," he explained, responding to her look of inquiry. "I thought you were going to tread all over my toes."

"I may yet," she said, smiling. "Of course I can dance. I have four sisters! But Vanessa and I were accustomed to taking the gentlemen's roles, so I have to keep reminding myself that it would be extremely improper to put an arm around my partner's waist or kiss his hand at the conclusion of a dance."

"I would not mind," he said generously.

The set passed off smoothly except for the part when Lydia was supposed to turn right in a circle with the other three ladies while the gentlemen turned left. Lydia automatically turned left to follow Edward, throwing the set into confusion. After that, Edward gave her a gentle nudge in the right direction when the pattern was repeated.

"It is so hot," she said when the set was over.

"You do not have a fan," Edward observed.

"No. Amelia lent me one of hers, but I forgot it."

"There is time for a glass of punch before Lowell claims you for the next set." He took her arm in his. "I shall leave you with Mrs. Coomb and fetch one for you."

"How kind of you, Cousin Edward," she said. Then she turned toward the door and gave a pleased gasp of surprise.

"There are Vanessa and Alexander! And *Mother!* What are they doing here?" She tugged Edward's arm and started to pull him in the direction of the newcomers. He gently extricated himself.

"Do you know, Lydia," he said sheepishly, "I think this might be a trifle awkward." She gave him a surprised look. Then enlightenment dawned. She had gotten so accustomed to Edward's company that she no longer thought of him as the enemy. From the look on Alexander's, Vanessa's, and Mrs. Whittaker's faces, though, it was apparent that they did.

"Ashamed to be seen with me, cousin?" Lydia said challengingly.

"You know I am not," he replied, sounding exasperated. "I have been promenading with you along Marine Parade for these two weeks. I just hoped to save you an awkward scene."

"Nonsense. What can they do at a public ball?"

"Well, unless I am much mistaken, I would venture to say that your brother-in-law would very much like to draw my claret."

Robert unexpectedly appeared at Lydia's elbow. He must have overheard part of their conversation, because he gave Edward a smug look and offered Lydia his arm.

"Acute of you, Lieutenant Whittaker," he said, grinning. "Let us find out what they are doing here, Lydia. Blakely probably has enough control not to plant the lieutenant a facer in public, but your mother looks as if she would dearly love to ring a very loud peal over someone's head."

Men, Lydia thought in disgust. Robert could not have chosen words more likely to shame Edward into accompanying her to meet her relatives. Edward's strong jaw hardened.

"Perhaps it would be best, Cousin Edward," she said hastily. "Please be good enough to tell Lieutenant Lowell that I will be with him directly."

"I will escort Lydia to him," Robert said, deliberately fuelling the flames.

"Stop it," Lydia commanded him. "Cousin Edward?"

"As you wish," he said, leaving them with a slight bow.

"Since when are you so friendly with that fellow?" Robert demanded under his breath. He had a welcoming smile on his face for Lydia's relatives, but his grasp on Lydia's arm was a bit tighter than was comfortable.

"If you leave bruises on my arm, I am going to give you *such* a clout!" Lydia whispered back. She felt Robert's hold relax.

"It would not be the first time," he said with a grin. Lydia did not miss the enraptured looks on the ladies' faces as they passed, and she gave an internal chuckle when she reflected that they probably were wondering what such a magnificent specimen of manhood saw in a plump, insignificant little creature like her.

Robert had brown, almost black, hair and a wide-shouldered, slim-hipped physique. His cornflower blue eyes sparkled with humor.

Lydia, for all that she had been disappointed at the age of twelve when Robert turned his boyish infatuation toward Vanessa, was so accustomed to his looks that she rarely gave them a thought except at times like these, when other women were making spectacles of themselves by drooling over him.

"Mrs. Whittaker," Robert said warmly as he took the older lady's hand. "I am surprised to see you."

The distraction—if distraction it was meant to be—failed miserably.

"It looks as if I have not come a moment too soon. Lydia! What were you doing with That Woman's son!" she demanded.

"Dancing, actually," Lydia replied matter-of-factly.

"How *could* you associate with the son of my greatest enemies? They cast us out of our home barely a month ago."

"Why are you here, Mother?" Lydia asked, deciding it was time to counteract her mother's interrogation with one of her own.

"We have come to take you to London tomorrow. Alexander has offered us the use of the town house he rents in the city for the little season. Is that not kind of him?"

Lydia's heart sank. Mama's renewed acquaintance with her favorite shops could only result in making further inroads into Alexander's purse.

"But I thought we were going to spend the fall and winter in the country supervising the repairs to the dower house. Where are Alexander and Vanessa going to stay if we take over their town house?"

"We will stay at Stoneham House with Lord Stoneham and Lady Letitia," Vanessa interjected. "Mama and the girls need new clothes, and so do you."

"More new clothes? But we just bought new clothes in Brighton."

"They are all very well for Brighton and for the country, but they would hardly do for London," Vanessa said, shocked.

"Where did you get that awful gown?" Mrs. Whittaker interrupted when Lydia was about to ask why not. "It looks as if it was designed for a woman of forty!"

"Mrs. Coomb *very kindly* lent it to me," Lydia said, summoning a bit of steel to her voice. "Otherwise, I would not have been able to come to the ball tonight."

"Really, you look very well, Lydia," Vanessa interjected hastily. "We must keep this shade of blue in mind when we go shopping. It brings out the color of your eyes so beautifully."

"Are you afraid you might hurt my feelings by telling me what a hopeless dowd I look?" Lydia asked, raising one eyebrow. "I have become quite accustomed to it, I promise you.

What time are you calling for me tomorrow? I want to be sure to have my packing done."

"At about ten o'clock, if that is convenient," Alexander said. The poor man had been standing there with a frozen look on his face during the whole of this uncomfortable conversation. Alexander had not flinched, if the dispatches returned from the Peninsula during the late war were to be believed, when faced with the prospect of charging the French army at the head of his regiment, outnumbered almost threefold. Public skirmishes between females, on the other hand, had the power to reduce him to petrified silence.

"I will be ready," Lydia said with a cool smile. "Mr. Langtry, I see Lieutenant Lowell waiting for me."

Robert offered her his arm and barely restrained his laughter until they were out of earshot.

"Bravo, Lydia! It is time you spoke up for yourself."

"I am so pleased," she said with a smile on her face for the benefit of Lieutenant Lowell as he approached to claim her for the next set, "that our little family squabbles provide you with entertainment, Robert."

He bowed rather too elaborately than the occasion merited and handed her over to the lieutenant.

Lydia was in equal parts embarrassed and relieved to see that Edward apparently had told his friend about Lydia's disruptive habit of absentmindedly taking the gentleman's part in the dance, for he unobtrusively gave her shoulder a nudge in the direction she should go as Edward had.

I am not going to think about tomorrow, she told herself determinedly as she enjoyed the music, the colors of the other ladies' gowns, and the pleasant experience of dancing with a personable young gentleman.

London.

Lord, how she hated London!

SIX

Edward felt helpless as he watched Lydia talk to her mother. It was obvious from Lydia's defiant posture that she was receiving a rare scold, and it was all Edward could do not to rush to her defense.

As if *that* would not make everything worse. He was certain Lydia would inform him in no uncertain terms that she could take care of herself perfectly well without any help from him to fan the flames of her mother's temper.

And she would be right.

How ridiculous. He felt like some overage Romeo losing what little sense he had over his Juliet. In spite of everything, he had to stifle an inward chuckle at the thought of his sensible Lydia cast in the role of that languishing female. Then he caught himself up short.

When did he start thinking of Lydia as *his?*

But after a moment of reflection, he realized it was true.

Lord, what a coil! He could not think of any woman in the kingdom whom his parents would find more unacceptable as his bride. They were willing to indulge him in just about anything, but marriage to *That Woman*'s daughter was not one of them. Especially not when the exquisite Lady Madelyn Rathbone and her huge fortune was, if his parents were to be believed, his for the asking.

Later, Edward watched Quentin and Lydia dance until he was

satisfied that his friend was adequately keeping Lydia from embarrassing herself by disrupting the circle. By then it was too late to solicit a partner for the dance, so he decided to go off in search of refreshment.

It would not do to make a cake of himself by staring at Lydia all evening, much as he enjoyed the little furrow of concentration on her brow as she tried to mind her steps, the way she blushed when the movement of the dance caused her partner to take her hand or put his arm around her waist, and the way her eyes sparkled with childlike pleasure when her partner sent her into a sedate spin.

Edward knew it was time to walk away when he started having murderous thoughts about Quentin for bringing that flushed look of exhilaration to her eyes. He knew very well Quentin was hopelessly besotted with Amelia Coomb!

He passed the chairs where the matrons were ranged, and flinched a little under the blistering look of hatred Lydia's mother directed at him. Edward had intended to ask Lydia for another set of dances, but he decided he had better not. Aunt Annabelle looked as if she would dearly love to stab him through the heart. The last thing he wanted to do was cause Lydia more discomfort.

Lydia's pretty brunette elder sister cast an apprehensive look at her husband, who looked as if he had been turned to stone.

At first, Edward thought Lord Blakely was glaring at him with that basilisk stare. When he realized that Alexander's eyes were glaring at a point beyond him, he turned to see the last people he had expected.

Oh, Good Lord.

His parents and Lady Madelyn Rathbone. Unless he was mistaken, the gentleman accompanying them was Mr. Kenniston, Lady Madelyn's guardian.

The presence of these individuals together in Brighton could only mean one thing.

They were here to promote a match between Edward and

Lady Madelyn. Edward manfully resisted an impulse to run when the four of them bore down upon him with determined smiles fixed on all their faces.

Uncle Henry and Lady Margaret! What were *they* doing here? Lydia barely heard Robert's stifled cry of pain when she trod heavily upon his toes.

"What the deuce," he began, forgetting his company. Then he stopped moving altogether.

"Lady Madelyn," he breathed.

Lydia gave him a sharp poke in the ribs to get him moving again. She remembered how Robert had made a cake of himself by flirting with the spoiled beauty earlier that summer. He and Alexander had nearly come to blows over it, thanks to Alexander's unendearing habit of designating himself the protector of every female connected with his family.

Not that the little hussy needed protection from anyone, Lydia thought bitterly as she watched the calculated way the flame-haired Lady Madelyn fluttered her lovely long eyelashes at Edward. As if feeling her eyes upon her, Lady Madelyn looked straight at Lydia and gave her a look of unmitigated venom.

Of course. Lydia was dancing with one of Lady Madelyn's admirers. Lady Madelyn, Lydia knew, considered every eligible male in England her personal property until she had indicated that she had lost interest in him and graciously permitted him to pay court to less worthy females.

"Lord, she is beautiful," the enraptured Robert whispered. "Whenever I see her after a long absence, I am dazzled all over again by her."

"Do stop hanging your tongue out like a drooling dog, Robert," Lydia said tartly. "You look like a lovesick idiot."

"Who would bother to look at me when such beauty is in the room?" he asked in a voice made husky with emotion.

Lydia gave Robert a look of utter disgust, and was relieved

to see the little smirk on his face that indicated he was teasing her. He might be a hopeless fool where Lady Madelyn was concerned, but it was a good sign that he had not lost his sense of humor.

With a gasp of recollection, Lydia looked for her mother. It would not do at all for that wronged lady to meet Uncle Henry and Lady Margaret in public.

Lydia watched Edward make conversation with his parents and another elderly gentleman with their party. His mother smoothed the sleeve of his dress uniform possessively. Then he offered his arm to Lady Madelyn with the obvious intention of taking her down to the dance.

Lady Madelyn and Edward made a dazzling picture with her glorious red hair shining like a beacon against the background of Edward's dashing dark blue uniform coat. In addition to that remarkable red hair, the statuesque Madelyn was blessed with lovely emerald green eyes, flawless gardenia-petal skin, and a wardrobe that would rival a Princess Royal's. Tonight she was wearing an ivory gauze gown embroidered with tiny crystal beads that shimmered when the light caught them. Lady Madelyn spoke many languages because of her travels with her diplomat father. She was accomplished in all the arts of painting and fancy needlework, and her singing voice, according to her besotted admirers, rivaled that of the great Madame Catalani.

Sick with jealousy—Lydia did not spare herself the self-loathing of calling this unworthy emotion by its real name—she watched Edward incline his head to listen to something Lady Madelyn was animatedly saying to him.

By now Lydia and Robert had disgraced themselves by colliding with another waltzing couple. They murmured apologies and stood by the side of the ballroom until the next set was forming.

"That fellow," Robert said in accents of loathing, glaring at

Edward as if he would dearly love to murder the current recipi-
ent of Lady Madelyn's practiced arts.

Men, Lydia thought in disgust.

Outwardly Edward returned Lady Madelyn's smiles and
guided her in the steps of the waltz; inwardly he thought desperately of escape. The smug looks of satisfaction on his parents' faces during their brief conversation had told him that as
far as they were concerned, his imminent betrothal to Lady
Madelyn was a certainty. Her guardian was here, obviously, to
meet him and give his approval to the match. Mr. Kenniston
would not travel to Brighton in order to meet a candidate for
his ward's hand whom he did not consider a serious suitor.

He glanced at Lady Madelyn.

Yes, she was beautiful. A fellow would have to be blind not
to acknowledge it. She was also clever and vivacious. Edward
always had been attracted to females with a bit of spirit. A
month ago he would have been perfectly willing to court the
lady.

A month ago he had not become reacquainted with Lydia.

Edward knew Lydia was close by, drinking a cup of lemonade
in the company of that bounder, Robert Langtry. Edward had
an unerring instinct when it came to Lydia that gave him as
much pleasure as it did anxiety. He could practically feel her
presence in any room.

"I assure you, Lieutenant Whittaker, I would not have known
you," Lady Madelyn was saying with a charming flutter of her
lashes.

"Nor I, you," he agreed absently. He almost laughed at the
sudden pucker of Lady Madelyn's brow, knowing very well that
he was expected to tell her that she was even lovelier than she
had been when he saw her last, and his heart would have known
her anywhere, or some such rubbish.

Madelyn was a pretty, self-centered doll whose sunny smiles

suddenly turned to frowns unless everyone in the room paid her the attention she considered her due.

Lord save him from being buckled for life to such a woman! Yet, he would not have much choice in the matter if the principals involved—not himself and Madelyn, but his parents and the guardian—agreed on the match. Edward's future was entirely dependent upon his parents' goodwill and that of his paternal grandfather, the earl, who would withdraw his financial support of Edward's expensive career as a cavalry officer without a qualm if Edward did not accept with proper gratitude the match that had been made for him. At the moment, Edward was the earl's favorite grandson and stood to inherit much of his personal fortune when the old man died and was forced to leave his title and entailed property to a remote cousin. But if Edward married to displease the old man, he knew his grandfather's largesse would come to an abrupt end and he would designate another of his male relatives as his heir.

"A man looks so different in a military uniform, I find," Madelyn said. "And your mustache is very dashing."

She gave him a provocative look from under her lashes.

"I have never been kissed by a man with a mustache before," she added with a coy little smile.

Well, you are not going to be kissed by one now, Edward vowed silently as he escorted her to his parents.

The orchestra was about to play another waltz. Madelyn stood on the sidelines, wielding her ivory-sticked fan of painted chicken skin against her slightly perspiring face. About to accept an invitation to dance by a young man who presented himself before her, she found herself abruptly snatched away from him by a grim Robert Langtry. He positively dragged her to the dance floor.

She looked back into the astonished eyes of her would-be partner and gave him an apologetic little smile.

"Mr. Langtry! What do you think you are doing?" Madelyn demanded, secretly thrilled by this masterful side of one of her favorite admirers. Robert was a delightful companion, always amusing and attentive. But sometimes being worshiped so devoutly became a bit tiresome.

There was nothing worshipful about his manner now. He stalked toward the dance floor on those long, muscular legs of his and made not the slightest concession for her smaller limbs.

"Robert," she whispered. "I am all out of breath!"

Her companion gritted his teeth and slowed down, but he did not smile or apologize. Nor did he answer her original question.

Once on the dance floor, he yanked her unceremoniously into his arms and glared down at her with the most forbidding expression on his face. Madelyn felt her heart flutter to think of Robert being so rough—and with *her!*

"What is *he* to you?" he demanded once the dance was in progress and he was propelling her around the floor in the steps of the waltz.

"I do not know who you mean," she lied.

"Whittaker. Do you mean to have him?" He gave her a hard little shake when she did not answer. "Do you?"

He almost pulled her off her feet with the force of the next turn in the dance and had to tighten his grip on her waist to keep her from falling.

"My guardian favors his suit," Madelyn said, so excited by the dangerous light of anger in Robert's eyes that she neglected to mention that Lieutenant Whittaker personally had not indicated the slightest wish to marry her.

Madelyn's guardian had refused several offers for her hand, but her spurned suitors had put aside their disappointment and begun paying court to other young ladies with unflattering speed. How sincere was their regard for her if she could be dismissed from their minds so quickly?

She once had had hopes of Alexander Logan, discerning at once the passion that simmered beneath that urbane surface.

But he regarded Madelyn much in the light of a younger sister and had married, to her disgust, Vanessa Whittaker, a penniless little nobody from Yorkshire.

It had not been easy to keep an unconcerned smile on her face and wish Alexander and Vanessa happiness when she was aware of the eyes of all the *ton* fixed upon her for signs of the vapors.

Robert was, he unabashedly admitted, an earlier suitor to Vanessa's hand. But from the moment he'd met Madelyn, he'd made it clear that his heart would be hers forever. Words that seemed like fustian rubbish on another man's lips seemed fresh and poetical on Robert's.

"Robert, do not be angry with me," she said soothingly. He looked down at her and the wounded look in his eyes made her heart melt. "The match is only something being discussed by his parents and my guardian. Lieutenant Whittaker has not offered for me yet."

"He looks so deuced impressive in that uniform," Robert said glumly.

"I think the mustache is especially intriguing," she could not help saying. The look of despair on his face made her repent at once. "Forgive me, Robert. I am a beast for teasing you. Do not worry about Lieutenant Whittaker. He does not seem to care for me above half."

"I cannot believe that," he said warmly.

Madelyn favored Robert with her prettiest smile—she practiced it in the mirror, so she knew its effect was devastating. When the dance was over and he suggested a walk in the hotel's lighted gardens, she did not object.

"London," Lydia sighed to Amelia as she finished packing her belongings. "How I hate it!"

"Hate London?" asked Amelia, round-eyed with surprise. "London is the most wonderful city in the world."

Lydia smiled at her young cousin and her heart swelled with affection. Amelia was such a sweet girl. So innocent. So hopeful. To Amelia, London was a city full of excitement. It was in London that Amelia would go to balls and parties, wear beautiful clothes, and, once she had enjoyed her season, marry Lieutenant Lowell in a tasteful ceremony at St. Paul's for several hundred guests.

"I was not happy there," Lydia said, feeling guilty about the cast-down look on Amelia's face. The last thing she wanted was to spoil Amelia's pleasure in anticipating her London debut. "But remember, I had not been presented yet when I was in London last year, so I could not go to parties."

"That is true," Amelia said, brightening. "It is all different for you now."

"Yes," Lydia agreed glumly.

Mrs. Coomb's maid appeared in the doorway, looking flustered.

"Miss Coomb, Lieutenant Lowell and Lieutenant Whittaker have called. My mistress is not yet dressed. I do not know what to do."

"Miss Lydia and I will see the gentlemen in the parlor," Amelia said, jumping up from where she had been seated on the bed and smoothing her skirt.

"Would that be proper, miss?" the maid asked uncertainly.

"Of course," Lydia said. "The gentlemen have been here dozens of times. If Mrs. Coomb does not mean to leave her room, perhaps you will come into the parlor after a few moments and sit quietly just inside the door. That way Mrs. Coomb can be assured that we did not meet the gentlemen without being adequately chaperoned."

"Very good, Miss Lydia," the maid said, her brow clearing. The woman stood aside so Amelia and Lydia could precede her from the room.

"I admire you so, Lydia," Amelia whispered, taking Lydia's hand in an affectionate grasp.

Lydia gave a snort of disbelief.

"You admire *me?*" she asked as they went down the steps. "Whatever for?"

"You always know what to do," Amelia said earnestly. "I could not have borne it if Quentin—Lieutenant Lowell, I *should* say—was turned away from the house just because Mama is still lying abed. I could not have prevailed upon Mama's maid to let us see them."

"Do not be absurd," Lydia said, giving Amelia a quizzical look. "I was only being practical."

"That is precisely why I admire you. You know how to do all sorts of practical things. Cook. Mend clothes. Butcher chickens."

Butcher chickens?

Lydia had to laugh at Amelia's earnest tone.

"Now *there* are accomplishments that would hold the occupants of any drawing room spellbound!" she said dryly.

"How do I look?" Amelia whispered as they arrived at the doorway to the parlor.

"Charming, as always," Lydia assured the younger girl.

"You look very nice in your new traveling dress," Amelia offered, making a minute adjustment to the frill at the throat of Lydia's blouse. It was one of the costumes Vanessa had purchased for her, and Lydia scolded herself for being pleased that Edward would see her in it.

As if he would be impressed by your new traveling costume when he spent last night dancing at the Castle Inn with Lady Madelyn. It had not escaped Lydia's notice that Edward had danced with the flame-haired beauty twice.

The gentlemen stood when they walked into the room.

"I hope you will forgive us for coming so early," Edward said, taking Lydia's hand. "I, that is, we wanted to see you before you leave for London."

"Thank you, Cousin Edward," Lydia said.

"As it happens, we will not remain in Brighton much longer

ourselves," Lieutenant Lowell said, looking at Amelia when she gave a little squeak of alarm. He placed a reassuring hand over hers for a moment before he continued. "We are being stationed in Romford in Essex next month."

"Why?" cried Amelia, looking bereft. Lydia knew Amelia had talked her mother into spending an extra two weeks in Brighton just so she could have more time with Lieutenant Lowell.

"Because we are needed," Lieutenant Lowell replied. "This is a soldier's lot, I am afraid."

When Lydia first came to Brighton she was convinced that Lieutenant Lowell was merely amusing himself with a pretty girl while stationed at the seaside resort. But it was now apparent to all but the most insensitive eyes that he was very much in love with Amelia Coomb.

In all that time Lydia had not seen him even look at another young lady, which was unusual fidelity for a personable young man who, like any of the dashing 10th Hussars, could have his choice of any number of besotted young lady tourists.

And Amelia all of a sudden aspired to domestic skills that included the butchering of chickens. No doubt she pictured herself as one of the heroic officers' wives who accompanied their men into battle to share their hardships and cook tasty meals for them of stringy fowl and pilfered vegetables over the campfires.

From the corner of her eye, Lydia could see Mrs. Coomb's maid enter the room and sit quietly in a straight chair by the door. Lydia gave her an approving smile.

"I will write to you every day, Quentin," Amelia said earnestly. Her eyes were bright with unshed tears.

"I should like that very much, Miss Coomb," he said as Amelia blushed for having been caught in the impropriety of using his Christian name again.

Feeling like an intruder, Lydia withdrew to the window to give the couple a bit of privacy.

"And how about you, Cousin Lydia?" Edward asked from so

close behind her that she could feel his breath on the nape of her neck. "Will you write to me?"

"If you wish," she said, pleased. "Of course, I shall have to smuggle your letters out of the house in my shopping basket to post them."

"Too true," he said wryly. "And if I wish to write to you, I will have to send my letters to Miss Coomb and have her send them to you under cover of her own."

"How ridiculous!" Lydia said, turning around to face him with a wry chuckle. "We shall be like Romeo and Juliet, which is quite absurd."

"Quite," Edward agreed, staring into her eyes. Amazingly, he reached out and touched her cheek. "I hope you will enjoy London, Cousin Lydia."

"Thank you, Cousin Edward," she said, forcing a cheerful tone to her voice. "And do be careful. I hear one meets up with quite desperate characters in . . . Romford."

"Yes. I might fall over a log in the dark while I am chasing smugglers," he said wryly. He looked out the window and narrowed his eyes. "We had best be off. I believe that is your brother-in-law, and he probably will be much better company on your journey if he does not see me here."

Lydia gave a long-suffering sigh.

"Alexander is not my father," she protested, "and I will not have him deciding who I shall or shall not see."

Edward gave her a smile that made her bones melt.

"My brave little cousin," he said fondly, taking her gloved hand and pressing it to his lips. "I could probably meet Lord Blakely without quaking in my boots, but I see your mother is with him and she positively terrifies me. Is there a back way I may slip out of?"

"Certainly not, sir!"

"I was afraid you would say that," he said, grinning. "Quentin, I suppose you must be my second if Lord Blakely challenges me for trifling with Cousin Lydia."

Amelia gave a delighted giggle, and Lydia felt her cheeks flush with sudden heat.

"How ridiculous! Even Alexander is not stupid enough to think there is the slightest danger of that," Lydia scoffed.

Edward pretended to twirl his mustache and leer at her.

"I would not be so sure, little cousin," he said.

When the housemaid appeared in the doorway, Amelia gave a nod and said, "Show Lord Blakely and Mrs. Whittaker in."

"Lydia, you are all packed and ready to leave, I hope," her mother said. Then she stopped dead in her tracks when she saw Edward.

"What is the meaning of this?" she demanded in an awful voice.

"My cousin Edward," Lydia said, "has *very kindly* called with his friend Lieutenant Lowell"—the officer bowed politely to the newcomers and they bowed back—"to wish me a pleasant journey to London."

"I see," Mrs. Whittaker said, fixing Edward with a stare that should have reduced him to a quivering mass of anxiety.

"Good morning to you, Aunt Annabelle," he said, bowing smartly. "And to you, Lord Blakely."

"Good morning, Edward," Lydia's mother said in a tone of voice that could cut ice. "Where are your things, Lydia? We must be going."

"I will fetch them directly," she said, turning to go upstairs.

Amelia put a hand on her arm.

"Sanders, please fetch Miss Whittaker's traveling case from her room."

Mrs. Coomb's maid stood, bobbed a curtsy and went to perform this task.

Lydia felt herself blushing. She never would get used to having servants underfoot to perform minor tasks that she could very well do for herself.

And being despised for never getting used to it.

"We shall miss Lydia so much," said Amelia, bless her, when the silence in the room began to be uncomfortable.

"And I am certain she will miss you," Mrs. Whittaker said, her expression softening briefly. "We shall all meet again in the spring."

Mrs. Coomb's maid came back into the room with the traveling case.

"I will carry it, Lydia," Alexander said in mild reproof when Lydia automatically reached for it.

"London awaits, my dears," Mrs. Whittaker said, giving Lydia a stern look that told her she was going to receive a piece of her mother's mind all the way to the city. "Please convey my thanks to your dear mother, Amelia, for her kindness to our girl."

Amelia and Lydia embraced briefly.

Then Mrs. Whittaker bent a frosty gaze on the two officers.

"Gentlemen," she said, giving a regal inclination of her head when they bowed to her. Then she grasped Lydia's arm in a firm grip and propelled her from the room.

Lydia was ready to sink. But when she looked back over her shoulder, Edward, far from looking affronted, gave her an outrageous wink.

But of course, she thought, irrationally cheered. He has a difficult mother of his own.

SEVEN

Edward had a far more uncomfortable meeting in store for him later that day.

"Mother, I cannot like the haste with which you and Father are promoting this match," Edward protested when his parents informed him that they had accepted an invitation on his behalf to meet with Mr. Kenniston in his suite at the Castle Inn. "Lady Madelyn and I have not exchanged much above a dozen words."

"Nonsense. You danced with her twice at the ball last night. She is a beautiful girl with the best of connections. What more do you need to know about her?"

"But we may not suit."

"Suit? *Suit?* The girl has a fortune of fifty thousand pounds in addition to the properties her mother settled on her. Of course you will suit!" his father shouted. "Do you think Lady Madelyn cannot have her choice of suitors?"

"Why is her guardian interested in a match with me for her, then? I do not even have a title, and I am told ladies set great store by them."

"You may thank my family connections for that, darling," Lady Margaret said with a superior smile. "Lady Madelyn's father and mine, both being earls, were great friends. Her guardian knows her father had a sentimental wish to see Lady

Madelyn and the grandson of his great friend joined in marriage."

"How ridiculous. He did not even know me."

"But he knew me and my family," Lady Margaret said smugly. "And I am known to be an excellent breeder of sons."

Edward could not help wincing. The mere thought of his dignified parents engaged in the activity to which his mother so indelicately referred had a tendency to make him queasy.

"But why the haste? She is still quite young."

"She will not remain on the market forever," his mother said, sounding exasperated. "You must make a push now! Last year I was afraid she would marry Lord Blakely, but he married the daughter of *That Woman* instead. I tell you, this is not an opportunity to be missed."

Well, Edward was as sensible of his own interests, he supposed, as the next man, but he had no intention of offering for Lady Madelyn.

It would be awkward, no doubt. His parents would denounce him as the proverbial Serpent's Tooth.

But Edward would meet with Mr. Kenniston and inform him that his parents had misunderstood his intentions with regard to Lady Madelyn.

When he was ushered into the elderly gentleman's presence, however, he noticed the clear brown eyes that regarded Edward from beneath a pair of beetle brows were not particularly welcoming.

"Be seated, young man," Mr. Kenniston told him with an imperious gesture toward a chair.

For a moment he stared at Edward in silence, an exercise that Edward might have found unnerving if he were a hopeful suitor to the lady's hand.

"I am told you wish to marry my ward," the old man said at last.

Edward opened his mouth to say he had no such intention, but he was silenced by another of his host's formidable stares.

"I have agreed to see you today as a courtesy to the daughter of the late Earl of Rathbone's friend. I am aware that Lord Rathbone and your mother's father often discussed the possibility of mingling their blood in the next generation."

Mr. Kenniston paused to fix Edward with another critical stare.

"You are a fine-looking young man, Lieutenant Whittaker. Madelyn may well be impressed with you. I imagine most young ladies are. I do not suppose you are aware that I was in military service once."

Edward waited a moment to see whether he was expected to reply. When it became apparent that he was, he murmured, "No, sir. I was not."

"It was the making of me," the old gentleman said reminiscently. "You would not think it to look at me now, but I was quite the war hero. The Royal 10th Hussars is a prestigious regiment with a proud history. The 10th performed honorably in the Peninsula. But *you* did not join the regiment until after peace was declared."

"No, sir," Edward admitted.

"Your grandfather tells me he was perfectly willing to purchase your commission for you as soon as you completed your education. Instead, you took lodgings in town and squandered your allowance on the pleasures of London."

"That is correct, sir."

"Why is that?" Mr. Kenniston asked in the tone of one who already knew the answer.

"My mother was opposed to my going to war," Edward said, offering the truth. "My grandfather—and I—yielded to my mother's wishes."

Mr. Kenniston gave a sour grunt of satisfaction.

"Do you always do what your mother says, boy?" He did not attempt to conceal the contempt in his voice.

"When I can," he said stiffly.

"As I said, I granted you this interview out of courtesy to

your parents," Mr. Kenniston said. "With Lord Blakely out of the running, I thought I owed it to them. Blakely is a man with a history of distinguished military service and he would have been able to make Lady Madelyn a countess someday. If he had offered for her, I would have accepted his suit with satisfaction. I hardly consider you an adequate substitute."

"At the risk of being discourteous, sir, I must point out that I have not made an offer. Your conversations were with my parents, and they were conducted without my knowledge or consent. Just as I suspect Lady Madelyn's opinion was not consulted in this matter."

"True. I will admit to you that I was prepared to reject your suit out of hand. But you have surprised me. You did not come strutting in here like a conceited popinjay and make your claim with all the confidence of a spoiled mama's boy convinced that every great honor should be his for the asking. Such a man would not do for Madelyn, for she has her father's determination in her, and she does not suffer fools gladly. Therefore, I have reconsidered."

"You *have?*" Edward blurted out in alarm.

"I am only rejecting your suit for the present." Mr. Kenniston stood and offered his hand for the first time in the interview.

Edward stood and accepted it.

"Return to your regiment, young man," the old man recommended heartily. "Distinguish yourself with hard service. Let it make a *man* of you, and I will be delighted to consider giving you my ward's hand in marriage."

Edward bowed solemnly and got out of the old gentleman's presence as soon as he could.

Lord, what a narrow escape! Now he could tell his parents with perfect truth that Mr. Kenniston had rejected his suit for the present. With the war over, he would have little opportunity to distinguish himself as a military hero. So he made his way to the Castle Inn to report the results of his interview to his parents, confident that the issue of his marriage to Lady Madelyn was now at an end.

London is an entirely different place when one has money, Lydia realized at once.

During Vanessa's London season in 1813, Lydia had been so busy caring for her younger sisters and worrying about putting food on the table that all she saw of London was the streets of shops catering to lower classes because their wares were all her family could afford.

Now the whole of the bustling city and its amusements were at her feet. Lydia was not permitted to go to balls because she had not been presented. However, she did not care in the least about going to balls.

Cousin Edward was with his regiment in Essex, after all, and there was not the slightest chance that he would dance with her in London.

Armed with a guidebook, Lydia took great pleasure in shepherding her younger sisters to the British Museum, to the Tower of London, and to Gunter's for ices. She enjoyed taking them as well for walks in Green Park. On these excursions they were often accompanied by Alexander and Vanessa.

"I hope you are comfortable in London," Alexander said, giving Lydia a friendly smile. "You are not too cramped in the town house, are you? It is rather small."

"We are very comfortable, I assure you," she replied.

"You are happy here, are you not, Lydia?" Vanessa asked, her eyes searching Lydia's face.

"Why, of course," Lydia said, amazed. "Why should I not be? You and Alexander have certainly spared no expense to keep us entertained."

"Well, you have always preferred the country—"

"And I still do. But this visit to London has been very pleasant for me, I promise you," Lydia said warmly.

Vanessa looked relieved.

"I am glad to hear it. I thought I detected a bit of melancholy in your manner, Lydia, and I was concerned. Robert Langtry is in town as well."

"Is he, indeed?" Lydia said, raising her eyebrows. "Should he not be at his estate, preparing for the harvest?"

"So one would think," Alexander said, his voice disapproving. "Instead, the silly gudgeon is haunting Stoneham House, making a cake of himself over Madelyn."

"Jealous, darling?" Vanessa teased.

"Hardly. It is just a cursed nuisance to be tripping over the fellow everywhere one turns."

"I do not understand," Lydia interjected. "Lady Madelyn is at Stoneham House?"

"I am afraid so," Vanessa said with a long-suffering sigh. "Lady Letitia invited her."

Lydia could imagine how dismayed Vanessa was to find a lady whom all the world had expected to marry Alexander as her fellow houseguest. Lord Stoneham and Lady Letitia had made it abundantly clear throughout their courtship that they would have preferred to welcome Lady Madelyn, and not Vanessa, to their family as Alexander's bride.

Poor Vanessa.

It must be the most uncomfortable thing in the world to marry a man whose relatives consider one inferior to them. Lydia decided she would rather remain a spinster.

"I will see if Lady Blakely is receiving," the haughty butler at Stoneham House told Lydia the following day when she came to return the single kid glove she had found under one of the chairs in the parlor and recognized as one belonging to Vanessa.

Just as if, Lydia thought sourly, Vanessa was likely to refuse admittance to her own sister. It was well in advance of the hour polite society deemed appropriate for paying calls, but Lydia was certain a more welcome caller would have been given a warmer reception.

Not that Lydia cared a rap. She would do very well without the approval of Lord Stoneham's toplofty butler.

After a moment, the butler showed Lydia into the parlor and told her Lady Blakely would be with her directly. Lydia did not anticipate a long wait. Vanessa always had been an early riser.

She picked up a novel that one of the ladies of the house had discarded, and was lost in the heroine's halfhearted struggles in the arms of a demonic villain when she heard a scuffle in the hallway.

"She will see me," a man's voice said vehemently. "She *must* see me."

"Lady Madelyn does not receive callers before one o'clock under *any* circumstances, sir," the butler insisted.

Lydia knew that voice.

"Robert!" she said, walking to the doorway of the parlor and peering into the doorway of the entrance hall. His face was haggard. "What is wrong?"

He turned a glassy-eyed stare on her.

"Lydia?" he asked, as if amazed to see her.

"Come in, Robert. Sit down."

The butler moved to stand between Robert and the parlor.

"Sir, I must insist that you leave at once. Lady Madelyn—"

"That will be *all,*" Lydia said sternly. "If you evict Mr. Langtry from the house, you will incur Lady Blakely's severest displeasure and consequently *Lord* Blakely's severest displeasure. Do you understand?"

The butler huffed off, no doubt to inform Lady Letitia that more of Alexander's unfortunate connections were making free of her parlor.

Lydia took Robert's unresisting arm, led him to the sofa in the parlor, and made him sit down.

"Robert! Tell me what is wrong this instant," Lydia demanded. She was seriously alarmed by his pallor. She sat down beside him and took his hand. It was as cold as ice.

"John is dead," he said bleakly. "God, Lydia. What am I going to do?"

"Your brother John? Robert! How awful! What happened?"

"Eleanor, too."

"His wife is dead, too? How can this be? Oh, Robert. I am so very sorry."

Robert took Lydia's hand in both of his and held on to it as if it were a lifeline.

"I am to take charge of the children. Thank God they were not in the carriage with their parents. And John's estate! I will have to manage it in trust for young Mark." He gave a short hysterical laugh. "Forgive me, Lydia. You must think me a madman. I cannot quite take it in."

"That is all right, Robert," Lydia said soothingly. "It is to be expected."

At that moment, Lady Madelyn appeared in the doorway.

"Robert?" she asked, squinting a little. Obviously she was not quite awake. "The butler said you were here, but I did not quite believe it."

"Madelyn!" Robert lunged to his feet and rushed to her. She gaped at his state of disorder.

"Whatever is wrong with you, Robert? Are you ill?"

"My brother is dead, Madelyn. Forgive me for intruding upon you at this early hour. I am not thinking quite clearly. I only knew I had to see you."

Madelyn looked from him to Lydia, completely at a loss.

"Come, Robert," Lydia said. "Sit down and try to tell us calmly what happened."

Robert came back to the sofa, bringing Madelyn along with him. Madelyn looked as if she would dearly love to escape from such an emotional scene. It was clear that she had no idea what to do.

What a little idiot, Lydia thought in contempt. Did Madelyn not realize that Robert had come to her for comfort, and she was not even coming close to rising to the occasion?

Robert took a deep breath and pulled himself together.

"It was a carriage accident," he said. "It happened just outside of London. John and Eleanor left the children in town with their nurse, and they were on their way to Lord and Lady Huntington's country house for a shooting party."

"Where are the children now?" Lydia asked.

"The children?" Robert repeated blankly.

"Robert!" Lydia said firmly. "This is important." She heard Madelyn give an affronted gasp when Lydia put a hand on each side of Robert's face and forced him to look at her. "Where are the children?"

Robert blinked.

"The children!" he said with a gasp. "They are at John and Eleanor's house with only servants to look after them!"

"I was afraid of that," Lydia said grimly. "Listen, Robert. The children must be frightened and upset. The bodies must have been brought home by now. You must go there *at once* and take charge."

"You are right," he said. "What was I thinking of?"

Lydia gave a sigh of relief. Alertness had come back into her old friend's eyes. He would do.

He rose at once, and he almost ignored Lady Madelyn completely in his hurry to get to his brother's poor orphaned children.

"Lady Madelyn," he said, blinking as if he suddenly had recollected her existence. He took her hand and kissed it. "I am sorry to fall apart like this all over your parlor. I do not know when I will see you again, so good-bye, my dear."

"What do you mean?" Madelyn asked, surprised. "Where are you going?"

Lydia tried very hard to keep the scorn out of her voice.

"Lady Madelyn," she said. "Robert has hundreds of details to see to. He must plan the funeral services, order mourning for the children and the servants, inform all the more distant relatives, and—"

"Oh, lord. I had not thought of all that," Robert said, his eyes widening with horror. "Lydia, come with me!"

"What? Robert, I—"

"Please! You are so much better at all of this than I am. You have met the children, and they like you. I have no wife to help me comfort them. Please say you will come. I cannot depend upon my mother, for she is devastated by John's death. He was her favorite, you know. And Eleanor's parents will be overcome with grief as well."

"Of course," Lydia said warmly. "I will do everything I can to help."

"Thank you, Lydia," Robert said gratefully. "I do not know what I would do without you."

"Well, let us go. The sooner we take those poor children in hand the better. Lady Madelyn?"

"Yes, Miss Whittaker?" Lady Madelyn said stiffly.

She is jealous, Lydia realized, recognizing the hurt look on the other woman's face. *She resents the fact that Robert has asked me, and not her, to help him through this crisis.*

"Will you please tell Vanessa what has happened and ask her to send my mother a note to inform her that I have gone with Robert to help with his brother's children? Oh!" Lydia reached into her reticule for the kid glove. "And give this to Vanessa, if you please. She must be missing it."

"Certainly, Miss Whittaker," Madelyn said, her eyes on Robert. "Mr. Langtry?" He took the hand she offered. "I am more sorry than I can say about your brother and his wife. Do let me know if there is any way in which I can help you."

Robert lifted her hand to his lips.

"Thank you, Lady Madelyn," he said formally. "But there is nothing you can do. I am sorry I disturbed you."

He offered Lydia his arm, and they were off.

EIGHT

When Madelyn called at the home of Robert's late brother and sister-in-law the following afternoon to pay her respects, she was not surprised to find *her* there.

Robert had come to *Madelyn* for comfort, not to Lydia Whittaker. It should be *Madelyn* at his side now.

But no. Lydia Whittaker had just poked her nose in where it was not wanted and taken charge of Robert and those dreadful children.

Madelyn had tried very hard to like the children for Robert's sake, but they did not pay the least attention to the presents she had chosen so carefully in an attempt to cheer them up and brought over to them earlier in the day. And whenever she tried to speak with Robert alone, they made conversation impossible with their insistent demands for their uncle's attention.

Lady Madelyn did not have a great deal of experience with children, but she usually got on well in a superficial way with the sons and daughters of her acquaintances by smiling at them a great deal and making much of them.

Robert's nieces and nephews cringed away from Madelyn when she tried to make friends with them, just as if she were some sort of child-eating monster.

Not that it was a bad idea, Madelyn thought wryly. She felt like a monster, feeling such resentment toward helpless children. Her place was with Robert, and Lydia Whittaker was there instead. The children seemed to like *her* well enough.

Flanked by masses of flowers, Robert and Lydia were stationed by the twin caskets with the children grouped between them as they received condolences from callers. Lydia was holding the youngest child's hand and had leaned down to whisper reassurances to him.

Matthew, Madelyn thought, recalling the child's name with some difficulty. It was hard for her to think of these children as individuals; she rather thought of them collectively, as one does a mob of vandals. The youngest was six and the oldest was twelve, *not* attractive ages in the least, as far as Madelyn was concerned.

They were all dressed in black, including Lydia.

Even though she was absolutely *nothing* to them.

The parlor, Madelyn observed, all too aware that she was deliberately looking for something to criticize, was draped with black crepe. A cold meal was laid out in an adjoining room, and the servants moved about with silent dignity, dressed in black livery.

All was exactly as it should be, Madelyn thought crossly. She knew Lydia Whittaker had orchestrated this dignified tribute to the deceased couple. How clever that drab little creature was to use Robert's family tragedy to ingratiate herself with him.

Lydia sank to her knees in a graceful sweep of black skirts in order to be on eye level with the little boy, who had started squirming and whining. Robert reached over and touched the child on the head. Then he gave Lydia one of the warm looks that he used to give only to Madelyn.

Madelyn fixed a smile on her face. She was not the daughter of a general for nothing; she *would* not lose her composure in public.

The line slowly filed by the caskets, and soon Madelyn stood in front of the chief mourners. The children drew closer to

Robert and glared at Madelyn as if they were joining forces against a common enemy.

Well, thought Madelyn, insulted. The feeling was *entirely* mutual.

The fleeting look of joy that crossed Robert's features when he saw her almost made up for it.

"Lady Madelyn," he said, taking her hand and giving it a warm squeeze. "How kind of you to come."

"Mr. Langtry," Madelyn said, returning the pressure of his hand. "I, ah—" She broke off with a slightly hysterical laugh and wanted to *die* of mortification. "Forgive me. I do not know what I can possibly say to comfort you. I cannot find the words."

"There *are* no words, my dear," he said softly. "Your presence helps more than I can say. Thank you for coming."

Madelyn had no choice but to press his hand again and move on. There was nothing she deplored more than the *gauche* tendency of some guests to monopolize the principals in a receiving line and bring it to a standstill. Madelyn exchanged a solemn nod with Lydia, and strained to summon a smile to her face as she greeted the children.

She might have spared herself the effort; they merely stared at her in sullen silence.

They have just lost their parents, Madelyn reminded herself, trying to be charitable. She was well aware that she was making excuses for them to avoid the simple fact that they did not like her. This was an unwelcome new experience for someone who had met with unquestioning approval and admiration most of her life.

And never before, she thought as her heart sank with despair, had anyone's approval been so important.

"Lady Madelyn, it is almost time for you to dress for the Swedish ambassador's reception," her companion whispered.

Elizabeth was merely an impoverished distant relative Madelyn's guardian had foisted upon her for propriety's sake, so Madelyn silenced the middle-aged woman with a frown. Madelyn knew the reception was to begin in less than two hours, but she could *not* leave yet.

She *had* to speak with him. Tomorrow he would accompany the children and their parents' bodies to his brother's estate for burial, and he would be gone a week at least.

"Follow me," she said to her companion.

She found Robert in a veritable circle of those encroaching Whittakers. Did they not leave him alone for a minute? Two clever-looking little girls were off to the side talking earnestly to Robert's nieces. A gawky adolescent was sitting between the two boys, obviously attempting to entertain them. She knew them at once as Lydia's sisters by their resemblance to her. The young people obviously were friendly with one another; the Langtry children looked almost amiable. Their guarded expressions snapped back into place as soon as they saw Madelyn approach their uncle. The youngest boy started clinging to Robert's leg, and regarded Madelyn with a face all puckered with ill temper.

"Here, Matthew," Lydia said, putting her arm around the boy and speaking to him in a firm, but not unkind, tone. "You have been very good, but now you are tired. Come away with us to the other room and have something to eat."

"I am not hungry," the child said, thrusting out his lower lip in a most unattractive manner.

"Well, *I* am hungry. You may come along to keep the rest of us company."

"Yes, Lydia," the child said, trustfully slipping his hand into hers.

"Thank you, Lydia," Robert said earnestly. "You think of everything!"

"Hardly," Lydia scoffed, giving him a quizzical look as she shepherded all the children from the room.

In spite of her dislike for Lydia and the way she managed things that were none of her business, Madelyn could only be grateful to her for taking the children away.

Robert gave her a brave smile that was so sad her heart melted.

"Come along, my dear," he said. "Almost everyone is gone, and I think we may go into the other room for a moment without flying in the face of propriety."

Elizabeth started to follow them, but Madelyn told her to stay behind.

Once they were inside what appeared to be a small salon, Robert closed the door behind them. Then, with a long sigh of relief, he drew Madelyn into his arms.

"God, how I needed this," Robert whispered into her ear. His arms trembled a little.

"I, too," Madelyn said, burrowing into the comforting warmth of his broad chest. He smelled of soap and bay rum.

"I hoped to say good-bye to you privately, for I may not see you for a long time."

"What do you mean?" Madelyn said, extricating herself from Robert's embrace to look into his eyes. "Surely you will return to London after the burial."

"I can hardly leave the children in the care of servants and come back to London straightaway to enjoy the rest of the little season."

"Why not?" snapped Madelyn. "They are not your children!"

Robert looked at Madelyn as if he had never really seen her before.

"That is where you are mistaken, Madelyn," he said quietly. "From now on, they are."

"Lady Madelyn," Elizabeth chided her. "It is hardly proper for you to call on a bachelor at his country estate."

"We will only stop for an hour."

"But Mr. Kenniston would hardly approve—"

"Mr. Kenniston will not know unless *you* tell him," Madelyn snapped. Elizabeth looked suitably cowed.

They were on their way to spend Christmas with a distant relation, an invitation Madelyn would have declined without hesitation had her hostess not lived in Yorkshire at so convenient a distance from Robert's estate.

She could not bear to be estranged from him any longer. The coldness in his face when she made that unforgivable blunder, demanding that he leave his grieving nieces and nephews to dance attendance upon her in London, had haunted her for two months.

Madelyn had her coachman stop to ask directions to Mr. Langtry's estate, and by mid-morning she had arrived on his doorstep. Robert's home, she saw, was a handsome red-brick manor in a nicely landscaped setting. It was rather smaller than she expected. All of her four properties, even her father's hunting box, were larger.

To her relief, the knocker was on the door. Robert himself walked around the side of the house before she could instruct her servant to use it.

"Lady Madelyn!" he exclaimed, his face flushed with pleasure. He put a casual arm around Madelyn's shoulders, which made Elizabeth frown, and ushered her into the house.

Thank heaven he was glad to see her! Madelyn would have been mortified otherwise.

"We are on our way to spend Christmas with Lady Woburn, who lives not twenty miles from you. I thought it would be a shame to come so close and not pay you a visit," she said.

"What a delightful surprise! Do come in. I shall ask the housekeeper to prepare some tea."

"That would be most welcome, Mr. Langtry," Madelyn said, smiling as Robert removed her wrap from her shoulders and handed it to a housemaid.

Bay rum, she thought, inhaling the fragrance of his cologne appreciatively. She could have wept for happiness.

"Lord, how I have missed you," Robert said under his breath while Elizabeth was occupied in handing her own coat to the housemaid.

He is going to kiss me here in the hall, right in front of prosy old Elizabeth, Madelyn thought exultantly. Only an idiot could fail to recognize the questioning look in his eyes and the way he had angled his face to align with hers. She felt her heart beat with anticipation as she lifted her face to give him access to her lips.

"Robert?" called the voice Madelyn had begun to hate more than any other in the world. "Has someone arrived?"

A moment ago Madelyn had been ready to throw herself into Robert's arms. Now she shoved against his chest so hard that he staggered.

"What is *she* doing here?" Madelyn demanded in a furious whisper as Lydia opened the wooden door that led to the rest of the house.

"Good morning, Lady Madelyn," Lydia said, her eyebrows raised. "How nice to see you. Do come in."

Just as if she had a right to act as hostess! Lydia smiled at Elizabeth and fell into step beside the older woman as Robert took Madelyn's arm and led her to a comfortable parlor. He seated her on the sofa and sat down beside her.

"I shall just go see about some refreshments, shall I?" Lydia said, smiling at Robert.

"If you please, Lydia," he said, smiling back.

"What is she doing here?" Madelyn repeated as soon as Lydia left the room. Robert gave her a surprised look, and Elizabeth made a little warning noise in her throat that Madelyn was too angry to heed.

"Lydia has come to help Mother and me with the children," he said, sitting back and stretching his long legs before him. "I thought it best to make it a rather small family party for Christmas this year."

"I had not heard that the Whittakers were members of your family," Madelyn said with an edge to her voice.

"No, but the loss of my brother has broken my mother's health, so Lydia has taken over the preparations for the holiday. She will leave us tomorrow to join her own family."

"How very *kind* of Lydia," Madelyn said dryly.

"Well, yes, it is, rather," Robert said, taken aback by the tone of her voice. "I do not know what we would have done without Lydia to comfort the children."

"Does she comfort you as well?" Madelyn supplied waspishly.

"Wherever did you get such a ridiculous idea?" asked Robert, giving her a quizzical look.

Madelyn got up and started pacing before the fire.

"Well, you can seem to talk of nothing else but dear, sweet Lydia and how *perfect* and *kind* she is!"

"Madelyn—" Robert held his hand out to her, but she was too angry to do more than snarl at him.

"*I* would have been perfectly happy to help you, but she had to butt in."

"Nonsense. Lydia has merely—"

"Wormed her way into your heart and assumed control over your household by taking advantage of your grief," Madelyn shouted.

"She has done nothing of the kind," he said softly, taking her shoulders and forcing her to look at him. "She *could* not, for there is no room in my heart for any woman but you."

Lydia stopped in the doorway, looking as if she did not know whether she should proceed or go back. At her heels were the children, who wore surly expressions on their faces when they saw who had come to visit.

"What is *she* doing here?" one of the older girls asked Lydia.

If Madelyn had acted like that in front of a guest when she was a child, she would have been punished. The earl had demanded flawless manners from his only child. But Robert did not even direct a look of reproof at the culprit.

"Lady Madelyn has come to visit us," Robert said mildly. "Is that not kind of her?"

The children looked far from gratified, but a servant arrived with a large tea tray before they could make any more unfortunate remarks.

"Please inform Mrs. Langtry that we have visitors," Lydia said to the servant.

"Begging your pardon, Miss Whittaker, but I was just up to the mistress's room and she was sound asleep."

"Ah. Well, do not disturb her, then."

The maid made a respectful curtsy and left the room; Lydia poured out the tea and one of the older girls handed it around. Madelyn could not help noticing how the children competed with one another for Lydia's approval.

Tears of humiliation stung Madelyn's eyes, but she refused to shed them. Every attempt to converse with Robert was interrupted by a boisterous demand for his attention on the part of one badly behaved child or another. Madelyn did not know how any rational person could bear it. Her nerves were all on end from their incessant prattling and giggling and jostling. She knew the insistent pounding between her temples was going to turn into a terrible headache.

When the tea had been drunk, Madelyn stood up and signaled Elizabeth to follow her example.

"We must be on our way," she said, regretting the loss of her fantasy that she and Robert could ever have a future together.

"Thank you for your hospitality," she added, clasping Robert's hand briefly. When prompted by Lydia, the children wished Madelyn and Elizabeth a pleasant journey.

Robert handed Elizabeth into the traveling coach, but he held Madelyn back when she would have followed her companion. He looked as miserable as she felt.

"Madelyn, my darling," He said. "Try to understand that I must put them first now."

"I *do* understand," she said, no longer able to keep her tears from spilling over. "I had just hoped—"

"Love, please do not cry," he said, brushing her cheek with a gentle fingertip.

Madelyn gulped and forced herself to smile.

"I brought Christmas presents for the children," she said, signaling one of her footmen to go to the boot of the coach and remove the big bundle of expensive toys that she had purchased with such optimism in London. She had pictured herself, Robert, and the children forming a cozy group by the fireside, opening the gifts that would prove to the children that she was not such an ogre after all.

"You did not have to do that," Robert said softly.

Madelyn felt like a fool.

"I know." She stood back as Robert accepted the parcel from the footman. "Do not tell the children who brought them. They will enjoy them more if they do not know they came from me."

Robert held his hand out to her. There was a look of suffering on his face that Madelyn knew was reflected on her own.

"Good-bye, Robert. I should not have come."

"I know," he whispered as he helped her into the coach.

Madelyn looked back at him until he was a small black dot in a blurred landscape of dead leaves and bare branches.

Between spending the little season in London and going to Yorkshire to help Robert Langtry get through the early days of mourning for his poor brother, Lydia did not see Alexander's country house until only a few days before Christmas.

Lydia realized at once that she had been misled by Alexander's description of it as a pretty little place in the country that brought him a tidy income.

"It is so *big*," she exclaimed when she entered the impressive hall. "It must require a fortune in coal to heat it!"

"Oh, Lydia," said Mrs. Whittaker with that little trill of laughter that grated on Lydia's nerves. "How like you to say such a thing!"

Lydia gave a little gasp of surprise when a housemaid took her traveling case out of her hand and held out her arm for Lydia's coat. She would *never* get accustomed to having all these strangers underfoot waiting to perform any number of trifling tasks. It seemed a great waste in servants' wages to her, but she knew better than to say anything.

Alexander's house was decorated with fragrant pine and holly in anticipation of the holiday. A tea table was set up in the parlor with an assortment of dainty biscuits and cakes on it, presumably in anticipation of Lydia's arrival. Her little sisters clustered around her, eager to tell her of the treats they had enjoyed in her absence. Alexander had bought them ponies, and he had also bought a saddle horse for Lydia. There had been visitors every day. And Mama had bought them more beautiful new clothes before they left London.

"We are going to put all our old things in a box for the poor," Aggie said virtuously.

"Oh, but for every day or playing outdoors—" Lydia began.

"Lydia, *darling*," Mrs. Whittaker said in the tone of one addressing a simpleton. "The girls can no longer run all over the neighborhood like hoydens. We owe it to Alexander to make a good impression upon his neighbors, and so our appearance must be above reproach."

"Mama says we never have to wear old homemade clothes again," Amy said gleefully.

"I see," Lydia said, putting down her teacup and standing up. "The girls are to be brought up to regard squandering Alexander's money as a virtue."

"Lydia, Lydia," her mother chided. "If Alexander does not begrudge the girls new clothes, it is not for *you* to object. And

I will just mention that the servants will think it very odd if you persist in performing tasks that are their responsibility."

Lydia looked down to see that she had stacked some dishes and wiped her side of the table with her napkin.

Later that afternoon, Lydia watched her mother and sisters fill two large boxes with clothes.

Lydia fingered the cherry-red ribbons of a dainty yellow dress she had made for Aggie at Easter last year. The cherry-red had cost more than the other ribbons because of its higher quality and fashionable color, but Lydia had bought it anyway because Aggie had seen the ribbons and wanted them so badly. Lydia had stayed up half the night stitching the dress and pressing it so it would be ready in time for Easter Sunday services. Now Aggie was perfectly willing to toss it into a box destined for the parish poor.

Lydia felt a lump form in her throat when she realized that her mother and sisters did not appreciate her years of hard work on their behalf any more than they appreciated that discarded dress.

She almost wished she had accepted Robert Langtry's invitation to spend Christmas with him, his mother, and those poor orphaned children. Mrs. Langtry was still prostrate with grief for her dead son and in no fit condition to be of comfort to her grandchildren or to Robert, who now was responsible for them all.

How foolish Lydia had been to think that her own family would feel slighted if she chose not to join them for Christmas. They were so delighted with their position of first consequence in the neighborhood, their new clothes, and the many luxuries Alexander provided for them that they would not have missed Lydia at all.

She had expected to lose herself in a whirlwind of activity in preparing the house for Christmas. But Alexander's efficient servants had taken care of everything, leaving Lydia nothing to do but sit by the window, stare into the snowy landscape, and wish that her lofty new status as the sister-in-law of a viscount permitted her to do something useful.

NINE

London
March, 1815

"Sometimes, Lydia Mary Whittaker, I do not understand you!" Mrs. Whittaker fumed as she paced the carpet in front of the white fireplace in Lydia's room. "You could attach him if you made the least push!"

It was some measure of her mother's agitation, Lydia reflected, that she was venting her annoyance in front of Monique, the superior maid Alexander had engaged to serve Lydia during the season, and on such an important evening.

Lydia looked with foreboding at the plume of seven white ostrich feathers that the maid was in the process of securing in Lydia's hair, *de rigueur* for ladies being presented to Her Royal Majesty Queen Charlotte at a drawing room. Lydia could think of nothing more likely to make her look ridiculous.

"Mother," Lydia said, trying to be reasonable, "Robert Langtry does not love me. Robert does not even admire me except as a nursemaid for his poor brother's children."

"Nonsense! He has been most attentive!"

Lydia gave a long-suffering sigh.

"Of course, he has. I am one of his oldest friends, and I have no choice but to listen as he pours out his longing for Lady

Madelyn into my unwilling ears. Believe me, no other woman exists for him."

"He would not be the first gentleman to look elsewhere once the object of his desire has become unattainable! Her guardian will never permit her to marry Robert Langtry. Their fortunes are too unequal."

"Oh, *Mother*," Lydia said, rolling her eyes. "I rather doubt that a gentleman with his heart fixed on Lady Madelyn is going to settle for me as second best, not with all the debutantes in London to choose from."

"But not too many of them would be content to live in the country for most of the year, coddle Robert's mother, and assume responsibility for his brother's children. That is where you have the advantage."

"You do make the prospect sound irresistible," Lydia said with a wry grin.

"Go ahead and laugh, missy," Mrs. Whittaker chided her. "You will be sorry when you are all alone in the world."

"Mother, there is hardly any danger of that," Lydia said, frowning when Monique produced a little pot of rouge and started applying it to Lydia's cheekbones with delicate strokes. The maid gave Lydia a look of mild reproach, and Lydia uttered the rest of her comment without moving her lips in deference to the unspoken rebuke. "I imagine there will always be a place for a lady willing to nurse other women's children and humor crotchety invalids. One's life is much the same whether one marries a person in need of these services or merely accepts a salary from him."

Mrs. Whittaker looked ready to explode, so it was fortunate that Monique created a diversion by reminding them of the business at hand. She was too well trained to let her exasperation show, but Lydia could tell this artist was shocked by her employers' failure to give the ritual of readying a young lady for her appearance at court its proper respect.

Lydia suspected she was as much of a disappointment to Monique as she was to her mother.

Finished with the elaborate coiffeur, the maid removed the protective cape from around Lydia's shoulders and signaled for her to stand. Lydia was not deceived by the woman's impassive expression or superior manner. Gossip about Mrs. Whittaker's hope of seeing Lydia married to Mr. Langtry would be all over the neighborhood by morning.

"Miss looks quite beautiful, if I may so," Monique offered, smiling at the figure in the full-length cheval glass that Lydia hardly recognized as herself.

Like all court dresses, this gown was cut to bare the shoulders and expose what Lydia considered rather too much bosom, which Lydia's mother had filled in with most of the jewelry that she and Vanessa between them possessed. The bodice was decorated with small crystal beads that glistened in the light, and the skirt was puffed out over a hooped skirt and several elaborately embroidered petticoats. Lydia felt rather as if the dress were wearing her instead of the other way around.

Still, it was made by a *modiste* of the first stare who had contrived in some cunning way to make the dress flatter Lydia's less than ethereal figure, and she was grateful.

Fortunately, the plumes that Lydia was so certain would look ridiculous, coupled with the elaborately curled coiffeur, added several inches of height and lent Lydia an odd sort of dignity.

"How amazing!" Lydia said, smiling at the maid who had labored so diligently to bring about this transformation. "You have done an excellent job, Monique. You may go to the servant's hall and have a cup of tea now. And do not wait up for me. We probably will be very late."

The maid smiled modestly in acknowledgment and curtsied before she left.

"Lovely," Lydia's mother said, putting her hands together ecstatically. "You look perfectly lovely."

"I would not go quite *that* far," Lydia said with a chuckle. "But I do not look nearly as frightful as I had feared."

After thinking of herself as being fat all her life, Lydia was pleased that her figure had improved greatly since the summer.

Lydia had spent the months of frustration at being forbidden the least useful occupation by taking long rides on horseback around Alexander's extensive property and, after they arrived in London, in Hyde Park. She and her younger sisters often took long walks in Green Park far earlier in the morning than was fashionable. In addition, her mother had insisted that she give up her beloved sweets in the interest of female vanity, with the result that her figure was a mere shadow of its formerly abundant self.

"A few more months on your reducing diet, and you shall look quite tolerable," Mrs. Whittaker said complacently.

"Not even to be a diamond of the first water am I going to stay on that wretched reducing diet for much longer," Lydia exclaimed. "Besides, we will be going into the country at the end of the season, so my new sylph-like perfection will be quite wasted."

"True," Mrs. Whittaker said coyly, "but we will receive visits from all of our old friends, including—"

"Robert Langtry," Lydia finished for her. "Mother, Robert is my *friend*. I could never reconcile it with my conscience to take advantage of his sorrow to manipulate him into marrying me. One must have some principles."

"Principles! Fiddlesticks!" Mrs. Whittaker grumbled. "Poor Alexander has spent a fortune on your come-out, and are you grateful? No, you are not."

"Oh, but I *am* grateful, Mother," Lydia argued. "I have enjoyed it ever so much more than I had expected."

"Then, act like it! All of Alexander's money will be wasted unless you make the effort to attract a husband."

"I am not going to work my wiles, such as they are, on poor Robert Langtry. That is final, Mother!"

"Stubborn girl," Mrs. Whittaker complained to the world at large. "Not like your sister."

"No, Mother," Lydia said with a wry smile. "I am not in the least like Vanessa, the perfect, the wonderful, the most beautiful and accomplished daughter, who has somehow managed to attain sainthood without going to the trouble of dying."

"Vanessa knew what was due her family. She was willing enough to marry *any* suitor, even Lord Omersley, who was old enough to be her grandfather and had not a tooth left in his head besides. And see what happened? She listened to her mother's advice and managed to attach a viscount!"

"Well, *bully* for Vanessa!"

"I have no idea where you got your stubbornness," Lydia's mother said in a voice of long-suffering. "It must be from the Whittaker side of your family, for it is obvious you do not take after me."

"No, indeed," Lydia muttered as she picked up her gloves and fan and left her mother to fume in solitude.

Edward had been in London for five days, but he and the members of his regiment had been so busy on official business that he despaired of seeing Lydia at all. He knew his duty in London would be over once the regiment was no longer needed to keep order in the chaos of the riots that had resulted from passage of the unpopular Corn Laws.

He did see Lydia's brother-in-law once. He had come out of Whitehall, and he and some of his more elderly colleagues had been hedged all around by rioters until Edward and his troop had dispersed the rabble so they could escape.

Lord Blakely had been knocked down trying to defend his companions from the mob's violence, and was half-reclining on the pavement by the time the soldiers had pushed the demonstrators back. Edward rode back to the fallen politician's side and dismounted. Lord Blakely was all alone; the men he had sought to defend had abandoned him without a moment's hesitation once nothing stood between them and their waiting carriages.

"Are you hurt?" Edward asked, taking Lord Blakely's arm and helping him to rise. He had been hit with a stone, and his cheek was bleeding slightly.

"No," Blakely said, sounding annoyed as he put his slightly crushed hat back on his head. Then he squinted into Edward's face. "Lieutenant Whittaker? Is that you?"

"Lord Blakely," Edward acknowledged, visually scanning the area for more rioters.

"I am much obliged to you," the politician said grudgingly.

"Merely doing my job," Edward said curtly. "I suggest you cease with the pleasantries and leave the area at once. This is not a safe place for you."

Lord Blakely grinned. "Compared with the Peninsula, it practically exudes goodwill."

Edward gave a long sigh of exasperation. He was becoming very weary of enduring unsubtle jeers from veterans of the late war. Even the bugle boy from the 10th managed to impress upon Edward his superiority to a mere lieutenant who had yet to see action.

"It appears that you have left your saber at home, my lord, so perhaps you should exercise a bit of caution," Edward said dryly. "For your information, some of us consider keeping the peace to be as valuable a service to the nation as that of waging war."

Unexpectedly, Lord Blakely grinned.

"Point taken, Lieutenant." He raised his arm in a casual salute that Edward did not bother to return.

Edward mounted, wheeled his horse smartly about, and left Lord Blakely to see to his own skin, all too aware that the only reason he had gone to the gentleman's aid was Blakely's connection with Lydia. Inexplicably, his usually sensible cousin was fond of the fellow.

Edward had no time to waste on fools, even gallant ones who had distinguished themselves in battle. For Edward's part, peacekeeping duty with the 10th suited him quite well. He enjoyed riding in formation with a column of well-trained men at his back, and he had always told himself that fellows who could not wait to act as targets for the bloody French were idiots.

Besides, if he *did* manage by some mischance to distinguish himself, Lady Madelyn's guardian might decide he was an acceptable match for her after all and *then* the cat would be flung among the pigeons.

Tonight he and his troop should have been at liberty. Unfortunately, the rioters' anger had not abated over the past week, so the men of the 10th had been called upon for some additional guard duty.

Queen Charlotte was receiving at a drawing room, and some feared the rioters might seek to do violence at St. James's Palace.

Consequently, Edward and the rest of his men were standing guard in front of the palace and at discreet stations inside. The royal family did not wish to dignify the rabble's efforts by making the additional security obvious, so the decision was made to augment the House Guards with members of the Royal 10th Hussars instead of regular members of the British Army. In their distinctive blue uniforms and tall fur hats, the members of the 10th would appear to be an honor guard for their colonel, the Prince Regent, who was expected to attend the drawing room, instead of a military force.

Edward tried not to yawn as carriage after carriage yielded its cargo of nervous debutantes with their elaborate gowns and feathered headdresses. Edward thought they resembled agitated swans awkwardly trying to negotiate their way across unfamiliar land.

He was staring straight ahead, allowing his eyes to rest by going slightly out of focus, when he saw the tips of some of those feathers wave right in front of him. Startled, he glanced down to see Lydia looking up at him with a grin on her face.

She walked all the way around him and ravished his senses with the faint fragrance of lily of the valley scent that he always associated with her.

"Lydia, come here at once!" hissed her sister Vanessa from the walkway into the palace. "What are you *doing?*" Another lady, whom Edward recognized as Lord Blakely's aunt, Lady Letitia, gave Lydia a stern look of disapproval.

Lydia waved a hand before Edward's face, and he almost lost his composure. The little minx knew very well he was obliged to keep his face expressionless while on guard duty, and she was trying to make him laugh.

It was so good to see her, even though he was possessed of a strong desire to turn her over his knee!

She looked so pretty with the beads on her dress and the jewels at her throat sparkling in the glow of the carriage lights, and her hair pulled up to reveal the graceful curve of her neck. Her beautiful eyes glowed with mischief.

Edward wanted to take her in his arms and tell her how wonderful she looked. Instead, he tore his gaze away from her laughing face and stared resolutely ahead.

"You will pay for this when I see you next, little cousin," he said in an ominous tone from the corner of his mouth.

"What will you do?" she asked. "Arrest me?"

"Worse. I am going to kiss you until your ears ring," he said softly.

"I beg your pardon?" she sputtered.

Edward hazarded a look at her face from the corner of his eye. She looked so adorably discomposed that he almost cast his duty to the wind to make good his threat then and there.

"Lydia!" commanded her sister with steel in her voice. "Come here *now!*"

Edward heard only the retreating scurry of slippered feet as his fair tormenter left him to his lonely duty.

* * *

He was so unbearably handsome, Lydia thought in despair as Vanessa and Lady Letitia shepherded her inside the palace to mingle with all the other visitors at court in the long gallery. She should have been anxious about the impression she was going to make on the queen, but Lydia's head had no thought to spare for such mundane considerations while her mind was full of Edward.

What a fool she had been to think he could ever regard her with any emotion stronger than friendship! And she had behaved like a perfect ninny, teasing him like that while he was on duty. Whatever had possessed her?

She did not dare to think of the softly whispered threat that made her cheeks flush with sudden heat.

He is making fun of you, the mocking voice that lived in her head told her. *You have only yourself to blame if he regards you with contempt.*

Lydia dreaded to think what her mother would say when she learned of Lydia's behavior. She could tell by the look on Vanessa's face that she would not remain silent. The nervous giggles of the other debutantes grated on her ears as she awaited her summons to the Presence Chamber.

"Miss Lydia Whittaker," announced the queen's lord-in-waiting after an eternity.

Lydia took a deep breath and stepped forward.

"Lieutenant Whittaker!"

Edward blinked and looked at the anxious young soldier standing before him.

"What is it?" he asked, forbearing to remonstrate with the man for leaving his post until he had heard his reasons.

"Private Lewis is white as paper, sir. I think he is going to swoon."

The last thing Edward needed was for one of his men to faint dead away in the queen's drawing room. His commander would have an apoplexy at the mere thought.

"Martin," he called to his second in command. "Take over here. I will send Lewis out." He turned to the man who had brought the message. "Return to your post."

"Yes, sir," the young soldier said.

Edward and the soldier marched into the palace and had a word with the House Guard on duty at the entrance to Presence Chamber. The soldier returned to his post, which was close to the doorway. Lewis, Edward could see, was indeed in dire straits. Unfortunately, he was stationed quite near the queen.

Edward squared his shoulders, walked as unobtrusively around the perimeter of the room as he could, and told Lewis to take a post outside. The man, following the same circuitous route Edward had taken, staggered slightly, and Edward was vastly relieved when Lewis was out of the queen's sight. A moment later, Lydia appeared in the doorway.

Exhibiting a composure that astounded him, she let down her train and waited for it to be spread out by the attendant. Then, when her name was announced, she walked slowly to the throne and curtsied before the queen.

"You are Lord Blakely's sister-in-law," the queen said kindly after Lydia had kissed her hands. "Quite an estimable young man."

"Yes, Your Majesty," Lydia said.

"I had the pleasure of receiving your sister last year, and I see she and Lady Letitia are with you today." She inclined her head graciously toward Vanessa and Lady Letitia, who were standing at the back of the room after having seen their protégée admitted to the queen's presence.

"I am, indeed, fortunate, Your Majesty," Lydia commented.

When the queen nodded but seemed to have no further comment, Lydia rose and curtsied again to the queen and to the Prince Regent, who was seated near his mother. As was customary, she backed all the way out of the room facing the queen.

It was considered a grave breech of court etiquette to turn one's back on royalty. When she reached the doorway, she looked straight at Edward and gave him a triumphant smile.

Edward let out the breath he had not realized he was holding.

Lord, he was proud of her! For the rest of the boring term of his duty, his mind was alive with schemes for getting his little cousin alone.

TEN

Lord Stoneham and Lady Letitia were hosting a ball in Madelyn's honor at Stoneham House, and everyone who was anyone was bound to be there.

However, Vanessa hardly had expected to see her mother's archenemy, Uncle Henry, and his insufferable wife, Lady Margaret, disporting themselves among the well-dressed guests in her father-in-law's house.

She caught her husband's eye as he stood near the receiving line having a conversation with one of his former commanders. The intimate smile that he kept for Vanessa alone faded when he saw the expression on her face.

"Darling, what is it?" he asked after he had excused himself from his companion and rushed to her side.

"Uncle Henry and Aunt Margaret are here! If Mama sees them—"

"Do not be concerned," Alexander said shrewdly. "There is such a crush of people here that they probably will not meet, and if they do, I doubt that they would make a scene with so many cursed respectable people present."

Vanessa could not help smiling. Alexander had resigned himself to attending fashionable parties as a necessary part of his government post. That did not mean he had to like them.

"That is better," he said, cupping his wife's face in his hand and leaning close. "Lord, I love that dress on you, but I love it even more *off* of you. Let us leave the matter of the warring Whittakers to Aunt Letitia and retire to our rooms for the evening. No one will miss us."

Vanessa gave him a sharp rap on the shoulder with her closed fan.

"It was worth a try," he said regretfully. "I suppose, then, that you had better be on the watch for your mother and Lydia so you can warn them that the other Whittakers are here."

He looked at his exquisite aunt, who was smiling and greeting guests, and his eyes narrowed.

"*I* am going to have a little talk with Aunt Letitia," he added.

As he expected, Letitia was all wide-eyed innocence when Alexander demanded to know why in blazes she had invited his mother-in-law's greatest enemies to the ball.

"Why, darling, did you not know that a match is being considered between Madelyn and their son, Lieutenant Edward Whittaker of the Royal 10th Hussars?"

"*That* fellow!" Alexander said with loathing. "I suppose you have invited him, too."

"But of course. As Madelyn's godmother I must avoid any slight to her future family by marriage."

"Even if it offends *my* family by marriage?"

Alexander rarely spoke to Letitia in that low, dangerous tone of voice, and it made her compress her lips in annoyance, heedless of the wrinkles such a rash action might cause.

"Your father and I have been as *nothing* to you ever since you fell under Vanessa Whittaker's spell!" she cried.

"Her name is Vanessa Logan, and we shall leave her out of this discussion, if you please."

"Now, darling. I have the highest esteem for dear Vanessa. But that ghastly mother of hers!"

"Mrs. Whittaker is a gentle soul who has been much wronged by her late husband's family. Are you aware that only last year Henry Whittaker threw her out of the home her husband brought her to as a bride?"

"Really, Alexander, you are always so unfair to me," Letitia said, dabbing her eyes with her lace handkerchief and taking care not to let this operation smear her artfully applied rouge. Letitia had the happy ability to cry real tears at will—a useful skill when one wanted to get one's way with the stubborn men in her family—but she declined to employ it in this instance. It would hardly do to return to the ballroom with reddened eyes and nose.

"Spare me the histrionics, if you please, Aunt Letitia. You have been moved by nothing, in this instance, but a delight in annoying my mother-in-law."

"You wrong me, Alexander, as usual," Letitia cried. "Have you no pity for poor Madelyn, pining away for that country squire she has fancied since last season?"

"Pining away? *Madelyn?*" Alexander said with a bark of rude laughter. "The little minx is out there flirting outrageously with every man in the room. She was even flirting with *me,* and she knows how pointless *that* is."

"Only because she is so desperately unhappy! You know I am not one to cast stones, dear, but if you had not taken up with Vanessa, she never would have met the wretched man."

Alexander gave another rude bark of laughter.

"Acquit me, if you please, of promoting a match between Madelyn and Robert Langtry. As I recall, I threw him out of the house the first time I caught him in the parlor casting languishing looks at her."

"Only because he offered for Vanessa once."

"Reason enough," Alexander snapped.

"Can you think of *nothing* but Vanessa?" Letitia said impatiently. "The ball is for *Madelyn,* and I cannot think of anything more likely to mend her broken heart than a new suitor for her to think about. Edward Whittaker is so eligible in every way! Apart from being quite excessively handsome, he will inherit not only his father's fortune but also his maternal grandfather's personal fortune."

"Very well," Alexander said, somewhat mollified. "I suppose I can see why you thought you had to invite him. But if I catch him sniffing around Lydia, I am going to throw him out the window."

Letitia gave a silvery peal of laughter. More than one of her besotted admirers had compared it to the clear, lovely notes of a bell.

"Lydia Whittaker?" she said incredulously. "Darling, your fondness for Vanessa's sisters has blinded you to reality. A young man of looks and fortune would hardly waste his time on a sharp-tongued young lady who has neither beauty nor fortune to recommend her."

"When I was in Yorkshire to escort Lydia to Brighton, he was quite attentive to her," Alexander said grimly.

"I will admit the girl is much improved since last year, but what man in his right mind would look twice at her when Madelyn is in the same room?"

"A man bent on causing trouble, of course," Alexander said grimly. "If that young jackanapes thinks he is going to amuse himself at the expense of a respectable young lady under my protection, he is *much* mistaken!"

"Nonsense!" scoffed Letitia.

"Perhaps. But all the same I am going to be keeping a careful eye on Lieutenant Whittaker," Alexander declared.

Lydia and her mother had just been announced when an excited Amelia Coomb came running to greet them.

"Amelia!" Lydia exclaimed, kissing her cousin on the cheek. "How pretty you look."

Amelia's delicate pink gown trimmed in frothy white tulle and embroidered lace made her look as if she were made of spun sugar. Her blond hair was swept up in a bouquet of curls crowned with pink roses, and her eyes glowed with happiness.

"Thank you, Lydia. Your gown is quite lovely. Who would

have thought you would look so nice in yellow? Few ladies can wear that precise shade."

"Never mind that," she said, drawing her cousin aside. "What has happened, Amelia? Have you seen Lieutenant Lowell?" Only the lieutenant, Lydia knew, could bring that glow of happiness to Amelia's face.

"No, but your cousin is here, and he brought me a message from him. We are all to meet tomorrow in Green Park. You *can* contrive to get away, can you not? Oh, *please* say you will come! My mother will hardly permit me to go walking in the park with two gentlemen and no lady along."

There was a vast difference between meeting Edward and his friend informally in Brighton with the approval of her hostess and sneaking behind her mother's back to see him in London, but Lydia did not hesitate.

"Of course I shall come."

"I *knew* you would not fail me! Ah! I see your mother and mine have found one another. And look! There are Lieutenant Whittaker's parents! Your cousin introduced Mother and me to them earlier, and they seemed very pleasant."

Lydia let out a gasp of pure horror as she saw the crisis unfold before her eyes. She picked up her skirts and ran for the scene of confrontation, only to find she was a second too late.

"Mr. Whittaker! Lady Margaret!" Mrs. Coomb said, greeting the couple when they would have turned away. In her innocence, she was impervious to the chill that suddenly descended upon the group. "How delightful! As you see, I have just been speaking with my cousin Annabelle, who is related to you by marriage, I understand."

The smile on her face froze when she stopped speaking and realized that both Henry Whittaker and his wife were staring right through their sister-in-law as if she were invisible. For her part, Mrs. Whittaker's face had turned an alarming shade of purple.

Lydia realized that her own friendliness with Cousin Edward

naturally had caused Mrs. Coomb to assume the families were
cordial.

"I believe," Lady Margaret drawled, "that I should like a cup
of punch, Henry."

Horrid Uncle Henry favored the crushed-looking Mrs. Coomb
with a cool bow and prepared to escort his wife away without
acknowledging either his sister-in-law or Lydia. Lydia returned
her aunt's venomous stare with one equally malevolent. How
dare she give Lydia's mother the cut direct in the middle of a
crowded ballroom!

Lydia was about to give her aunt and uncle a much-deserved
piece of her mind when she felt a gentle touch on her shoulder,
and was displaced from her position in the uncomfortable little
circle to admit a fifth person.

"Mrs. Coomb. Mother. Father. I see you have found friends,"
Edward said, smiling at his parents.

He turned away from them before they could find words to
respond to this outrageous remark.

"Aunt Annabelle, it has been a long time," he added, kissing
a startled Mrs. Whittaker on the cheek. "You look well."

"How do you do, Edward?" Lydia's mother said, picking up
the threads of her dignity.

He smiled at her, then turned to Lydia and startled her very
much by taking her gloved hand in his.

"You look very pretty this evening, Cousin Lydia," he said.
"If you are not engaged for this dance, I hope you will give me
the pleasure."

"Thank you, yes, Cousin Edward," she said. She could have
kissed him for allowing her poor mother to save face. "That
would be very agreeable."

"Splendid. If you will permit me, Aunt Annabelle, I will
escort you to a chair and procure a glass of punch for you first."

"Thank you, Edward," Mrs. Whittaker said, taking the arm
he offered her.

Lady Margaret's eyes narrowed dangerously.

"Mother," Edward said to her. "I shall visit you tomorrow, if I may."

"Yes, Edward." Lady Margaret scowled at her cherished first-born. "I have much to say to you." With a cool nod to Mrs. Coomb and her daughter, she took her husband's arm and sailed majestically away.

"*Bless* you, cousin," Lydia said with a sigh of relief after they had found a chair for Annabelle and left her comfortably situated next to one of her friends. "I was afraid for a moment that Lord Stoneham's guests would be treated to the edifying spectacle of our mothers rolling on the floor and pounding one another like unruly schoolboys."

Edward gave her an arch look.

"It appeared to me, my dear, as if *you* were about to attack my mother."

"True," Lydia acknowledged with that mischievous little smile that made Edward long to kiss the corners of her mouth. "You saved me from disgrace as well."

"I should *hope* you are much obliged to me," he said ruefully, "for if I do not mistake the matter, I am in for a rare bear garden jaw when I call on Mother tomorrow."

"I wonder that you should risk such a terrible fate," Lydia said from the corner of her mouth as she made a curtsy to the opposite gentleman and held both arms out to him so they could circle sedately in the middle of the lines.

When she returned to her place at his side, Edward gave her a rakish grin.

"My dear, I would risk anything for you," he said.

The movement of the dance caused him to take Lydia's waist and circle with her, so she was a bit breathless when she replied.

"Take care, cousin. Your mother would *kill* you, never mind the bear garden jaw, if she heard you say anything so ridiculous," she said, obviously taking it as a joke.

Lydia did not have a vain bone in her body, Edward thought affectionately, even though she had grown remarkably pretty in the few months of their parting. He found her lack of artifice refreshing after being shamelessly pursued by all the young ladies of London on the catch for husbands with expectations.

When the dance was over, Edward offered Lydia his arm and suggested that they go in search of refreshments.

Instead, they found Lord Blakely blocking their path with a forbidding scowl on his face and his arms crossed over his broad chest.

"Good heavens, Alexander," Lydia said in genuine surprise. "Whatever have I done to bring that ferocious look to your face?"

"Lydia, I should like to have a word with Lieutenant Whittaker, if you do not mind," he said.

Edward nodded, and was about to declare himself at Blakely's disposal when Lydia stepped in front of him and faced her brother-in-law with her hands on her hips.

"I will not have Cousin Edward insulted simply because his parents tried to give Mother and me the cut direct," she declared.

"They did, did they?" Alexander growled, looking around ominously. "If I had known that—"

"Very *good,* cousin," Edward said with an amused chuckle. "That certainly improved matters."

Alexander's dark, dangerous gaze settled on Edward.

"It pleases you to trifle with me, sir, but I am warning you to take care," Blakely said coolly.

"Good heavens, Alexander," Lydia said, rolling her eyes. "You sound like the villain in a bad play. Cousin Edward rose magnificently to the occasion when his parents snubbed us. What more do you expect?"

"I think he knows," Alexander said, regarding Edward from narrowed eyes.

"He does, indeed," Edward said, allowing his eyes to narrow

as well. "And I take leave to tell you that your concerns are groundless."

"You are as bad as he is," Lydia told Edward in disgust. "What are you going on about? People are beginning to stare."

"You, actually," Edward said, replying to her question without taking his eyes off of Lord Blakely. "Am I not correct?"

"Perfectly," Alexander said.

"Will you stop this?" Lydia cried out in exasperation. "Alexander, you cannot seriously believe that Cousin Edward has designs on my virtue."

Edward burst out laughing at the expression on Blakely's face. He could not resist taking Lydia's hand and giving her gloved knuckles a lingering kiss.

"In your usual inimitable style, my dear, you come right to the heart of the matter," he told Lydia. "Take a damper, Blakely. I am not about to ruin my own cousin."

"See that you behave yourself," Blakely said with another one of those ominous looks, and took himself off.

"Well," said Lydia, staring after him. "That was very odd. Playing patriarch to my family has given him some very queer ideas."

"I fail to see," Edward said gallantly, "what is so surprising in the idea that I might be paying court to a lovely lady at a ball."

"Nothing at all! Just the idea that you might be paying court to *me.*"

Edward started to object, but he was suddenly compelled to grab Lydia out of the way when a distraught-looking man crossed their path and almost collided with her. The intruder wrenched Lady Madelyn out of her partner's arms while she was engaged in performing the waltz.

"Is that not your neighbor from Yorkshire?" Edward asked sharply as the man grasped Lady Madelyn's arm a bit roughly and dragged her off the dance floor.

Lydia gasped.

"Why, it *is* Robert Langtry. What is he doing here?"

"Making a fool of himself, it appears," Edward said coolly. Madelyn and Langtry were shouting at one another, although Edward was too far away to hear what they said.

When Langtry grasped Madelyn's shoulders and shook her hard, Edward sighed with annoyance and went to her rescue.

Madelyn wanted to burst into tears of frustration.

How could Robert *do* this?

She had missed him so much. He looked distraught and unkempt, as if he had been running his fingers through his hair.

Even so, she could hardly permit him to shove her about in this undignified fashion. Her coiffeur was quite ruined.

"I will *not* come away with you," she told him. "How can you suggest such a thing after the way you have behaved?"

"There must be a place where we can be private."

"There may be, but I am not going there with you!"

Lieutenant Whittaker, an intimidating figure in his dress uniform, took Robert by the arm.

"Lady Madelyn, is this gentleman bothering you?" he asked politely.

"Go away," Robert snapped drunkenly.

"If you have no further business here," the lieutenant said, "I suggest you permit me to accompany you to your carriage."

"Take your hands off of me," Robert demanded, resisting Whittaker's attempt to propel him from the room.

"Calm yourself, Langtry," Whittaker said in a perfectly reasonable tone. "If you do not have a carriage, I will find you a hackney."

Robert slapped the lieutenant across the face, and Madelyn could hear a collective hiss escape from half a dozen throats.

Whittaker closed his eyes for a moment and shook his head.

"I wish you had not done that," he said in a low, menacing

voice. Then he grabbed Robert by the scruff of the neck and marched him toward the door.

"Let *go* of me!" Robert snarled, trying to get away from him. *"Madelyn!"*

His anguished cry tore at Madelyn's heart, but she could hardly permit Robert to bully her in the middle of a ball! Thank heaven Lieutenant Whittaker had intervened when he did.

Madelyn stiffened when she saw that pushy little Nosy Parker Lydia Whittaker hurry to where the two gentlemen were struggling.

Who asked *her* to interfere?

"Darling, are you all right?" Lady Letitia asked anxiously as she put a comforting arm around Madelyn's shoulders. "Alexander," she added to her nephew, who had come to Madelyn's other side, "do procure a glass of wine for Madelyn. She looks a bit pale."

"No, Alexander, I thank you," Madelyn said, gently extricating herself from her godmother's embrace. "I am quite well."

"My poor dear. Imagine Mr. Langtry behaving in such a savage manner! I had not thought him quite so bad as that! You must be quite overset."

"Oh, yes. Quite," said Madelyn anxiously. "Lieutenant Whittaker will not hurt him, will he?"

"No. It looks as if Lydia will protect your precious Mr. Langtry's skin," Alexander said, his voice dripping with scorn.

Madelyn's head swiveled to where Lydia was earnestly talking to Robert. He still looked distraught, but after a moment he took the hand she offered to him and trustfully permitted her to lead him away. Lieutenant Whittaker followed a pace or two behind them. Madelyn watched them leave the ballroom as her heart seethed with jealousy.

"Here, old man, up you go," Edward said with false heartiness as he half-lifted, half-shoved a loose-limbed Robert into the hackney carriage. Lydia was grateful he had followed them, for she could not have managed Robert by herself.

Edward handed some coins to the driver. "Where are you staying?" he asked Robert.

"Wimpole Street," he muttered. "Could not find anything better . . . Could not bear to stay in John's town house . . ."

"Wimpole Street," Edward repeated to the driver, handing him some more coins. "See that he gets inside the right house safely, will you?"

"Yes, sir," the driver said.

"Capital," Edward said. "Pardon me, Lydia. I must close the door so your friend can be on his way."

"The lady is *Miss Whittaker* to you," Robert said belligerently.

"Hush, Robert," Lydia said soothingly. "You must go to your lodgings and go to sleep."

"Lydia!" Robert cried plaintively as Edward closed the door behind him with a resounding slam.

ELEVEN

Edward knew his interview with his mother would not be a pleasant one, but it was even worse than he had expected.

"How *could* you dignify that dreadful woman's pretensions by acknowledging her in my presence," Lady Margaret demanded as soon as the footman who had announced Edward left the room.

"That *dreadful woman* is my aunt, Mother," Edward said in a neutral tone. "And if I may remind you, your own sister-in-law."

"We do *not* acknowledge the connection," Lady Margaret said haughtily. "Particularly at a ball attended by all the most prominent members of the *ton* and your future bride."

"You can hardly call Lady Madelyn my future bride," Edward pointed out. "So far, all I have done is dance with her."

"But you did rescue her from being annoyed by that man who accosted her. I must say, my son, that you exhibited quick thinking there. I am certain Lady Madelyn was most grateful, and it is sure to make your suit more favorable to her."

"How very gratifying," Edward said dryly.

"The whole situation is intolerable! Who is this Mr. Kenniston to withhold his approval of Lady Madelyn's marriage to *my* son?"

"Well, he *is* the lady's guardian," Edward said, answering the rhetorical question and receiving a look of exasperation from his mother. "I suppose he can withhold his approval from any-one he wishes."

"And then, *then* you had to compound matters by making up to that mousy little daughter of hers."

Edward had no difficulty in following his mother's circuitous conversation. All roads, he thought wearily, always lead back to *That Woman.*

"You left me little choice after your behavior to Cousin Lydia and her mother." Edward learned long ago never to refer to *That Woman* by name. It only made Lady Margaret more livid. "They were connections of our host, after all."

Lady Margaret drew herself up to her full height, much the way a cobra does before it is about to strike.

"Do you *dare* presume to criticize my behavior?" she de-manded. "Lord Stoneham does not give the snap of his fingers for *That Woman* or her daughters, nor does *anyone* in our circle! I have been at tremendous pains to disassociate my family with her, which is no simple task when we share the same name. And now you have implied before the whole of the polite world that we acknowledge the relationship!"

"Good God, Mother. All I did was dance with Cousin Lydia. Once." He did not think it politic to mention that he gladly would have danced with her again, but that her mother looked as if she might have an apoplexy when he started to approach the place where she and Lydia were sitting together. He rather imagined that poor Lydia, from the look of Spartan endurance on her face, had been receiving a lecture similar to the one Edward was receiving now.

"So you only danced with her *once,* did you?" Lady Margaret said angrily. "That is not what I hear from my acquaintances who were in Brighton over the summer. Can you imagine how your father and I felt when we learned that our son was asso-ciating socially with *That Woman*'s daughter for almost a month? Do you ever give one thought to what you owe your name?"

"It is *her* name, too," Edward said rashly.

To his consternation, his mother gave a high-pitched shriek and looked as if she wanted to claw his eyes out.

"Yes, it is her name because That Woman *stole* him from me!" she cried. Her face was so distorted that Edward hardly recognized his well-bred mother in this harpy who suddenly confronted him. "George Whittaker was meant for me! Me! We were to be married. Then she worked her wiles on him and persuaded him to marry her instead!"

"Mother, I am so sorry," Edward whispered, putting his arms around her for comfort when she broke down into sobs. "So sorry."

She looked up at him with a tear-stained face. In all his life he could not remember his mother shedding tears.

"He was the only man I have ever loved," she said, resting her head against Edward's shoulder like a weary child. "Our betrothal had been announced. You cannot imagine the humiliation I had to endure in addition to the betrayal of a man I thought returned my regard."

"Hush now, Mother," Edward said soothingly. "This cannot be good for you."

"I married Henry soon after that," she went on as if she could not stop herself. "He was younger than George, but much like him in appearance. I thought I could *make* myself love him." Lady Margaret gave a bitter little laugh. "I do not believe the solicitors drew up new settlements. They merely substituted Henry's name for George's. It was a satisfactory arrangement for all involved—except me."

Edward heard a noise, and looked up to see his father watching them soberly from the doorway.

Lady Margaret regarded Edward with a determined look on her face, no less intimidating for the tears that were drying on her cheeks.

"I will see you *dead* before I see you married to That Woman's daughter," she said in a low, vehement voice. "She is not going to ruin your life the way her mother ruined George's and mine!"

Mr. Whittaker walked into the room and faced his son with an impassive look on his face.

"I will take care of her now," he said, gently turning Lady Margaret out of Edward's arms and putting a supporting arm around her waist. "Come along, now, my dear," he said softly to his wife. "I will see you in my study after I have made her comfortable, Edward, if I may."

"Certainly, sir." Edward watched his parents leave the room. Now he saw what had been hidden from him since childhood. With the self-absorbed blinders of youth, he had never seen his parents as real people who had once been young and ruled with passions as strong as his own.

Edward went to his father's study and thought, when Mr. Whittaker finally entered the room, that his father seemed to have shrunk into himself. He certainly looked more vulnerable than Edward had ever seen him in his life.

"I am sorry you had to witness that, Edward," Mr. Whittaker said, seating himself in a chair, facing his son with stoic dignity. "Your mother is an indomitable woman, but for her the pain of my brother's betrayal is still as fresh as it was all those years ago. I hoped the violence of her emotions would fade in time, but—" He paused and seemed to collect himself. "In short, you see now why we will never reconcile with Annabelle Whittaker."

"Well, it certainly explains why you threatened to send me to India two years ago when I merely mentioned that I had seen Cousin Vanessa at a ball and thought her quite pretty," Edward said wryly. "Would you have done it?"

"Probably not. Your mother would have stopped me. Despite the fact that she is not demonstrative, she loves you very dearly." He busied himself with one of the pens on his desk, as if embarrassed. "As do I," he added awkwardly.

Edward reached across the space that separated them and covered his father's hand with his.

"I know. I have always known," Edward said. His father clasped Edward's hand convulsively and then released it.

"I have seen the way you look at Lydia Whittaker. I do not understand it, but I have seen it. Please understand that I will do *anything* to keep you from marrying her for your poor mother's sake. If I have to disinherit you in favor of your brother, I will do it, even though it will break my heart."

"You love her that much?"

The look of stubborn resolution on his father's face melted like wax.

"I have always loved her," he said quietly. "When she agreed to marry me, I could not believe my good luck. George always had been the chosen one, a brilliant student when he was at university, a buck of the first stare when he lived in London, the strong, athletic one who made our father proud. And when it came time for him to take a wife, he became betrothed to Margaret, the most wonderful girl in the world. I knew she had been much attached to my brother, but in my youthful arrogance I had some romantical notion that I could make her forget him with the strength of my ardor, or some such rubbish."

He gave a shuddering sigh.

"Lord, I was a fool! Margaret never got over him, and the knowledge that he was as unhappy with Annabelle as she was with me made it even worse."

"Father—"

Mr. Whittaker made a gesture of denial.

"Do not interrupt, Edward," he said wearily. "You deserve to know the truth, and if I stop now, I will not be able to get through the thing. This is not . . . easy for me."

"I am sorry," Edward murmured, bracing himself to hear the rest.

His father gave an ironic little laugh.

"George drank himself to an early grave and quickly ran

through our father's fortune. But to his death he remained a fine figure of a man, while I grew fatter and grayer with every passing year. Fortunately, as second son I inherited my mother's fortune, and through judicious investments and careful management of the remaining lands I was able to return our family to its former prosperity. I worked hard to prove myself worthy of her, but she has never forgotten him." He gave a long sigh. "In my eyes she is still the most wonderful woman in the world. Pathetic, is it not?"

"Surely she loves you," Edward said. "She gave you six children."

"And four of them sons. A man could not ask for a more loyal or dutiful wife. I suppose she is fond of me," Mr. Whittaker said with an ironic little smile, "as one grows fond of some fat old dog that has been lying about the place forever. It is not quite the same thing, you will agree."

"No, I imagine it is not," Edward acknowledged cautiously.

"Edward, you must understand that my will and your mother's in the matter of your preference for Lydia Whittaker's society are inflexible. I have explained the consequences of your refusal to accede to our wishes."

"You have been quite clear on that score, sir," Edward agreed. "If you will excuse me, I must be on my way. The riots have become more serious, and I must be available if I am assigned to duty. And of course," he added with a deprecating laugh, "the queen or her daughter may require an escort on a shopping excursion."

His father stood and clasped his son's hand.

"Your mother and I are very proud of you," he said.

"I cannot imagine why," Edward said facetiously. "So far in my illustrious career I have chased a great many smugglers along the coast of Essex, outfaced simple men carrying sticks while I was on horseback with a saber of Toledo steel, stood guard at a great many excruciatingly boring ceremonials, and danced at a number of balls."

To Edward's relief, his father laughed and gave him a light cuff on the shoulder. Then he accompanied Edward to his horse and shook his hand before he mounted it. Edward looked back just before he turned onto the next street and saw that his father was still standing outside, watching him ride away.

Lydia had to laugh at herself. Here she was, pleasantly occupied in deciding what to wear for her excursion with Amelia, Lieutenant Lowell, and Cousin Edward, exactly as if she were one of those totty-headed females she had always despised.

Perhaps there were advantages to being an ornament of society, she thought, weighing the merits of a stylish pomona-green walking dress against those of an older, less fashionable ensemble of cobalt blue that the dressmaker had said was extremely flattering to her eyes.

The blue, she decided. When a lady has only one good feature, she must exploit it for all it is worth.

Her mother, she thought, would be proud of her for remembering that bit of sage wisdom from her own lips. She would be less pleased, however, to learn that Lydia was about to apply this practical advice in the cause of impressing Cousin Edward.

Lydia could not believe she was about to embark upon a clandestine meeting, for one could call it nothing else. She was about to change her clothes when a maid appeared in the doorway and announced the arrival of Robert Langtry.

Robert! Lydia was thoroughly ashamed of herself for letting the anticipation of seeing Cousin Edward send her childhood friend and his troubles straight out of her head.

She went directly to the parlor and held out her hand when he stood to greet her.

"Robert!" she said, appalled by his haggard appearance. "I am so glad to see you."

He took her hand in both of his.

"You must think I am the greatest fool living," he said ruefully.

"Hardly!" Lydia scoffed. "You are not the first man to make a cake of himself over a vain, overdressed doll and you will not be the last."

Robert gave a reluctant laugh, and his eyes almost looked normal for an instant.

"*Will* you always say exactly what you think?"

"Probably," she said calmly. "Sit down, Robert, and I will ring for tea."

"You are such a comfort to me, Lydia," he said, taking her hand again.

"I cannot imagine why," she said in a bracing tone. "Have you been drinking again? I cannot otherwise account for this rather maudlin effusion of sentimentality."

"Good God, no! I am sober as the grave, I assure you," he said, sounding offended.

"Well, that is a good thing. We cannot have you lurching about my mother's parlor. She would be quite shocked."

Robert actually laughed out loud.

"What a horrid girl you are!"

"There! That is more like it," Lydia said approvingly. She rang the bell and asked the maid to bring refreshments. "Now," she said when the girl had gone, "tell me what possessed you to present yourself at Stoneham House in such a deplorable condition last night."

"Lady Madelyn, of course," he sighed. "I miss her so much. I *had* to see her, so I left the children with Mother and came to town for the week. Lord, what must she think of me?"

"If you ask me, Lady Madelyn is too busy thinking of herself to spare any thought for you," she said dryly. "But do not let me interrupt. You were saying?"

Robert gave a long-suffering sigh.

"This is what I get for expecting sympathy from *you*," he said. "I did not receive an invitation to the ball at Stoneham

House, but I knew Madelyn would be there so I decided that I would send word to her that I was waiting outside and ask her to come speak to me for a minute. I will swear to you that was all I intended."

"Except," Lydia added helpfully, "you presented yourself in a thoroughly disguised condition, so the butler showed you the door."

"Crude, but essentially true," he said ruefully. "Not being quite myself, I decided to force my way into the ballroom."

He put his elbows on his knees and allowed his head to rest in his hands.

"I recall declaring my passion for her at the top of my lungs. Then I begged her to leave the ball and run off to Gretna Green with me."

"You must be joking," Lydia said, awed. "And I used to think you the dullest sort of boy when we were children."

"Dull? You thought me *dull?*" Robert said, digesting this as if it were a bitter pill. *"That* is a pretty thing to tell a fellow when he is down in the dumps."

Lydia threw up her hands.

"Robert, I said I *used* to think you dull. You are anything *but* dull now. Especially if you are going to make a habit of getting drunk and trying to abduct respectable young ladies from crowded ballrooms."

"Well," he said with a glimmer of his old humor, *"that* makes me feel better."

The maid came in with the tea, and Robert gave a sigh of relief as he sipped from the cup Lydia poured for him.

"An old friend is a wonderful thing," he said contentedly. "This morning I was ready to slit my own throat for being such an idiot. I still doubt that the love of my life will ever speak to me again. But after a few minutes of being abused by you, I feel almost like myself. I say, are those macaroons?"

"Yes. Cook bakes them often because my little sisters love them so."

"Where are the girls?"

"Out riding in the park with Alexander and Vanessa. Alex is quite determined to make little equestriennes of them all."

"And you do not like it."

Lydia looked at him with astonishment.

"Whatever do you mean?"

"You are jealous, Lydia," he said quietly. "I have noticed how much you dislike it when the girls make a fuss over Blakely. It is understandable, of course. You were responsible for them for so long."

Lydia sighed.

"Does it show so much, then?"

"Only to someone who knows you as well as I do. Blakely has a way of riding roughshod over people."

"The girls adore him, though. They quite think of him as an indulgent father because they were so small when Papa died. Although he has treated me with nothing but kindness, I cannot like the way he *assumes* he knows what is best for me and tries to tell me what to do."

Robert took her hands again.

"You are not happy here, are you?"

"I am not *un*happy," she said thoughtfully.

"It is not precisely the same thing, is it?" he asked.

"No," she admitted ruefully. "It is not."

Lydia gave him a sudden smile.

"Let us have no more of *that,* if you please. I am supposed to comfort *you,* not the other way around."

"And you have, my dear friend," he said affectionately. "What would I do without you?"

"Probably have a much higher opinion of yourself," Lydia said archly.

"True," he said, laughing. Then his face sobered. "Lydia, you are such a good sort of girl. If I were not in love with Lady Madelyn—"

Lydia gave a mild shriek and shrank away from him.

"For pity's sake, do not let my mother hear you say that! She will be off to Stoneham House to poison Lady Madelyn within the hour!"

"Your mother?" Robert said, looking confused. "Why should she do any such thing?"

"Robert, do not be dense. You must know that Mother has the forlorn hope that you are going to offer for me."

"Oh, my poor dear," Robert said, choking a little. "Has she been making your life miserable?"

"You know how persistent she can be once she gets an idea in her head," Lydia said. "Her primary ambition in life now that Vanessa married so well is to find a man for *me.*"

"He will be a fortunate man, my dear," Robert said softly.

"And you would not be in his shoes for the whole of Golden Ball's fortune," Lydia said, laughing.

"A fellow could do worse," Robert murmured as he took his leave.

When Lydia returned to the parlor after seeing him off, she found her mother seated by the tea table.

"Mother! I thought you had gone out," Lydia said, smiling at her. "Robert Langtry was just here. Why did you not join us?"

Mrs. Whittaker looked very sly.

"I thought you and your young man would be pleased to spend some time alone."

"Oh, Mother," Lydia said with a sigh. "I am going to change and go around to Amelia's house. I promised her I would walk with her in Green Park."

"All right, Lydia. Enjoy yourself," her mother said with a knowing little smile on her face.

Lydia smiled back, even though she strongly suspected her mother was enjoying a pleasant little daydream of marrying her off to Robert Langtry.

No matter, Lydia thought as she rushed upstairs to don her pretty blue walking costume.

Soon she would see Edward!

* * *

Lydia's smile of greeting faded when she saw Amelia's face. She turned to Lieutenant Lowell, who had risen when Mrs. Coomb's housekeeper showed Lydia into the room, and noted that he looked equally sober.

"Good afternoon," Lydia said cautiously. "I am sorry to be late."

She looked around the room.

Amelia's young man looked extremely embarrassed.

"Edward sent you this," Lieutenant Lowell said.

Lydia accepted the folded note and broke the wafer. The message contained an apology for not joining her on the excursion with Amelia and Lieutenant Lowell as planned. It was very formal, not at all typical of the friendly correspondence she and Edward had exchanged while he was in Romford.

"I see that Lieutenant Whittaker had another obligation," she said, looking up from the note. She was annoyed to see that her vision was slightly blurred. She had so counted on seeing him.

"We can still enjoy our walk," Amelia said, taking Lowell's arm.

"Certainly," Lydia agreed, forcing a smile to her lips.

Cousin Edward had never exhibited anything for her except a casual fondness. It was *she* who had been silly enough to attach undue significance to the sort of kindness one might demonstrate toward a virtual stranger.

She set off with Amelia and Lowell, determined to behave as if she had not a care in the world, even though her heart was breaking.

Edward had always thought of his mother as the personification of something cold and indestructible. A glacier or a diamond, perhaps. Seeing her so miserable shook his world, even though he had cut himself loose from his mother's apron strings years ago.

His head reeled at the thought of his mother in love with Lydia's father. His earliest memories of Uncle George were of a pathetic sot, old before his time and so cynical that Edward and his brothers were half afraid of him.

Edward's own father was a model parent in comparison. He was stubborn and dictatorial and a frightful snob, but he put his family first. George Whittaker frittered away his fortune on drink and gambling, and he left his wife and daughters virtually penniless upon his death.

Edward always had believed there was love at the foundation of his parents' marriage despite their rather cold politeness to one another in public. In their world, married couples did not commit the vulgarity of showing affection for one another outside their bedroom.

Now he knew that their seemingly sound marriage was a matter of making the best of an impossible situation. His mother still pined for a man who had been dead for years; his father had long ago given up hope that she would ever regard him with anything but duty and mild affection.

Both of them blamed George Whittaker—and now that he was dead, his widow—for their wretchedness. On the subject of George Whittaker's wife and daughters, neither of them was quite sane.

Until now Edward had been certain that he and Lydia between them could somehow heal the rupture in their family and find happiness together. Now he knew that was hopeless.

He wanted to see her; he could *not* see her. Not now. It was a coward's trick to send her a note instead of meeting her and telling her the truth, but he needed time to think their dilemma through.

Later that afternoon he found out that there would be *no* time.

TWELVE

Lydia, Amelia, and Lieutenant Lowell had just entered the gates of the park when their startled eyes beheld a scene of pandemonium.

"What in blazes is going on?" Lieutenant Lowell asked a passerby.

"He has escaped!" the man shouted. "Napoleon has escaped from Elba and raised an army on the mainland!"

"We will be murdered in our beds!" a woman shrieked. She almost knocked Amelia down in her panic, and Lieutenant Lowell had to steady her to keep her from tumbling to the pavement.

"Good God," Lieutenant Lowell said blankly. Recollecting himself, he took Lydia and Amelia firmly by their elbows, turned them around, and quickly started walking them away from the park.

"Quentin," Amelia asked, her pretty face alarmed. "Does this mean the war is not over after all?"

"I am afraid it does, sweetheart," he said. "I am going to escort the two of you to Amelia's house, because it is closest. I must return to the regiment at once. Miss Whittaker, I apologize for not escorting you home, too."

"I understand," Lydia assured him. "Do not worry about me. I will just walk home from here."

"Miss Whittaker! I could hardly permit such a thing," Lieutenant Lowell said, shocked.

"Well, you can hardly compel me to stay with you," Lydia said. "Really, Lieutenant Lowell. I can take care of myself."

Ignoring Amelia's pleas for her to stop, Lydia rushed for home. She knew her mother and sisters would be upset by the news, and she needed to be with them. Her mother was given to hysterics, so Lydia knew she would have the children convinced they were about to be eaten alive by the Gallic Monster if Lydia was not there to calm her down.

Lydia was doing quite well in negotiating her way through the crowded street full of people, many of whom were just standing stock still in stupefaction, when she felt both of her arms seized from behind.

When her struggles seemed ineffective in breaking her captor's iron grip, she raised her foot and tried to kick him.

"See here, my girl," chided a familiar voice. "That will be enough of *that!*"

"Edward!" Lydia exclaimed. When he loosened his hold on her, she whirled around, threw her arms around his waist, and buried her face in his breast.

"Well," he said, putting his arms around her. "This is more like it."

Lydia turned red to the roots of her hair. What must he think of her, throwing herself at him like that? He sounded amused. She wanted to die.

"I thought you were engaged elsewhere this afternoon," she said tartly, pushing him away. He took her arm and started walking.

"It was a lie," he admitted. When she would have wrenched her arm away from him, he tightened his grip. "Never mind that now. This is no place for a woman alone. Where are Quentin and Miss Coomb?"

"We got separated," Lydia said tartly, her mind whirling. He had lied about having another commitment that afternoon. He had not wanted to see her. "You do not need to escort me home. I can take care of myself perfectly well."

"Lydia, do not poker up on me," he said, resisting when she tried again to release herself. "I had good reasons for not wanting to meet you this afternoon, but they seem unimportant now. The regiment is leaving soon for Ramsgate. From there we will embark for the Continent. I do not know when I will see you again."

Lydia stopped dead in her tracks and stared at him in dismay.

"I have so many things to say to you," he said earnestly, "and there is so little time."

Yet they spoke very little on the way to Lydia's house because Edward set such a rapid pace that Lydia could not speak beyond a gasp. Threading their way through the traffic took all of their concentration.

A street away from the house, however, Edward startled Lydia by pulling her into his arms.

"I do not think it would be wise for me to walk boldly up to your mother's door," he said softly. He silenced her with a finger over her lips when she would have spoken. "No time for arguments, love. I know one is supposed to lead up to this sort of thing by slow stages, but—"

Then Edward kissed her, and the rest of the world just fell away. There was no other way to describe it. The warmth. The heat. The boldness of his lips and the slight, pleasant friction of his mustache on her sensitive skin. Lydia's heart was beating so fast she was certain he must hear it.

He gave a long sigh when they finally broke apart to breathe.

"You are the most surprising girl," he said softly.

When she looked down in consternation, he raised her chin with gentle fingertips so that he could look into her face.

"Lydia, I must go to my parents. They will be worried, and I do not know precisely how much time I have before the regiment leaves. But I want you to keep this for me while I am gone."

He reached inside his pocket.

"Take it," he said as he handed her a lady's ring of an antique style composed of three oval-shaped amethysts set in silver. It was a dainty thing, and it was a little worn at the back of the band.

"Grandmother's ring," Lydia said, awed. She remembered it from when she was small, before the branches of the Whittaker family had become completely estranged.

"She gave it to me before she died and told me to give it to the woman I would love someday. Grandfather gave it to her when they were young, and she was sentimental about it."

"But surely your mother—"

"Mother would have scorned it as being too insignificant for her notice, and Grandmother knew it. I have worn it on a cord around my neck as a talisman these many years."

"I cannot accept—" Lydia began, although she wanted this ring with all of her heart. It was so exquisite. And it had rested next to his skin. "It would be most improper—"

"I am only asking you to keep it for me until I return. It would give me pleasure to know that it will be yours if something happens to me."

"But—"

Edward silenced her with a butterfly-soft kiss.

"Indulge me in this mawkish bit of sentimentality, little cousin," he said, cupping her face in gentle fingers. He gave her a mischievous smile. "Every soldier likes to kiss a pretty girl before he goes into battle, and you appear to be the only pretty girl close at hand."

"How *very* flattering," Lydia said tartly.

He laughed, but his smile quickly faded.

"Seriously, Lydia, I would much rather know you have the ring than take the risk that some bloody frog will loot it from my dead body and give it to one of his doxies."

"Do not say such things," she cried, alarmed.

Edward took her hand and kissed it.

"We must get you home. While I am perfectly willing to face the French, your mother terrifies me. So, in true star-crossed-lover style, I shall conceal myself behind a tree and watch to make sure you are admitted to the house safely."

He took the ring from her hand, slipped it onto her finger, and gave her a kiss on the cheek.

"Be well," he said in benediction as he took her arm and turned her in the direction of home. The ring was a delicious weight on her finger, even though he had made it abundantly clear that it meant nothing.

Nothing at all.

As soon as Edward presented himself at his parents' town house, his mother started issuing orders. She did not even wait for him to be announced. She had been on the watch for him, and catapulted into the hall so quickly that the startled butler dropped his salver with a loud clang.

"Come into the parlor, Edward. Your father and I wish to speak to you. Where have you *been?*" she demanded. "I sent a note around to your lodgings an hour ago."

"I was out. Mother, I came to take my leave of you. The regiment will be mobilized at once for—"

"You are not going," she cried. "I forbid it!"

"Of course I am going," he said, shocked. "I must."

"You will sell out immediately, of course. I will *not* risk my eldest son in battle."

Edward's mouth dropped open. She really meant it.

"Mother, to do so would bring disgrace upon all of us. An officer does not sell out at the first sign of impending war."

"Do not be ridiculous!" she scolded. By then she had preceded him into the parlor and stationed herself next to her husband, who was standing before the fireplace. *"Tell* him, Henry!"

"My dear?" he asked politely.

Lady Margaret gave him a look of annoyance.

"Tell Edward that he is to sell his commission immediately."

Edward's heart sank. Henry Whittaker always did what Lady

Margaret told him. In this, however, he had underestimated his father.

"I am afraid not, Margaret," Henry said, looking very sad. "Not even for you."

Lady Margaret stared at him in disbelief.

"Henry!" she shrieked. "Edward is your heir. He is too valuable to be risked in battle!"

"Then you should not have encouraged your father to buy him a commission."

"But we thought the war was over! How were we to know those incompetent idiots would let Napoleon escape and go rampaging about the Continent again?"

"Mother," Edward interjected before Lady Margaret could unleash the full force of her wrath on his poor father. "I *must* go."

"Papa will not permit it," Margaret said with a smug smile of satisfaction. "I shall write to him at once, and he will put a stop to this nonsense."

"If the earl does as you wish, I shall be very much surprised," Henry said. "He could only despise a man who would turn his back on Mother England when she needs him."

"But it is *Edward* we are speaking of! My son!" Lady Margaret burst into tears and threw her arms around Edward, weeping hot tears all over the breast of his uniform. "My beautiful son," she sobbed.

"Mother," Edward whispered soothingly as he kissed her forehead and held her close. "It is my duty. I *must* go. I do not wish to give you pain, but—"

"Come, Margaret," Mr. Whittaker said sternly as he put his hands on her shoulders. "You must accept this with dignity for Edward's sake and your own."

Lady Margaret looked up into her husband's eyes and her face was alive with fury.

"Beast!" she cried, and struck him across the face. Her red

handprint stood out with ghastly starkness against the sudden pallor of his skin. "I *hate* you!"

Henry let his hands drop to his side and turned away.

Lady Margaret's face crumpled.

"Henry?" she said, touching his shoulder. "I did not mean it. Truly, I did not."

He turned and looked at her; his face was as cold as marble.

"Henry, *please!*" she cried desperately.

After a long hesitation, Henry opened his arms and she rushed into them, sobbing and murmuring inarticulate apologies.

Henry held her tightly, and his eyes were filled with profound sadness as he looked over his wife's head and into Edward's face.

"I must go," Edward said.

"I know, my son," his father replied. "I know. Take care, Edward, and come back to us."

Edward bowed.

"I will, Father. Good-bye, Mother."

But the distraught Lady Margaret could only cling to her husband and weep as if her heart would break.

The bracing salt spray made Edward's face tingle with cold as he faced the land mass veiled in fog that could be his doom, but all he could think of was the way Lydia had kissed him on that last, rushed encounter before his regiment set sail for Ostend and the theater of battle.

He should have spoken.

But what would he have said?

Marry me, Lydia. Even though all I can offer you is a life of scrimping and making do that will make your deprived childhood seem luxurious by comparison.

An irresistible proposition, Edward thought wryly. What woman could refuse the delightful prospect of marrying a man with no fortune who brings with him a pair of hostile in-laws into the bargain?

It was hopeless. Absolutely hopeless.

Edward jumped, a bit startled, when the pungent fumes of a cheroot reached his nose.

"Well, *that* is a relief," Lowell said, between puffs. "I would have tried to take your pulse in a moment."

The men looked out to sea in companionable silence.

"Amelia begged me to elope with her to Gretna Green last week," Lowell said regretfully.

"Good God!" Edward exclaimed, all the more shocked because he had almost begged Lydia to elope with *him*. "No gentleman with any regard for a young lady would do such a thing."

He had told himself the same thing with regard to himself and Lydia.

Lowell gave a long sigh.

"That is why I did not," Lowell admitted. "I offered for her, but her mother said she is too young to marry."

"She *is* only sixteen."

Lowell gave a snort of derision.

"Mrs. Coomb wants a title for Amelia, and she is waiting to see if a more desirable suitor will come forward before she commits her daughter to me."

"And so Miss Coomb begged you to elope with her."

"Yes," Lowell said with a long sigh. "I told her we would have little chance for happiness if we began our married life by alienating her mother."

"Well, that was probably true," Edward said, thinking how unhappy Lydia would be if marrying him meant she must be estranged from her mother.

"I told her we must wait until we could marry honorably. She cried so much I was alarmed for her. But I hardened my heart against her entreaties because I knew best." He gave a little snort of derision. "Now we are on our way to war and I may never see her again."

"You could not have known Napoleon would escape."

"No." Lowell gave a long, wavering sigh and looked back out to sea. "Tell me I did right, Edward."

"You did right," Edward said obediently, even though with the uncertainty of war looming over them, he was not so sure.

THIRTEEN

Hard work had always sustained Lydia through her troubles in her past, but her family's improved circumstances had relieved her of the routine household tasks that would have made the long wait for news of Edward's fate bearable.

Therefore, she was quick to volunteer her services when Robert Langtry brought his nieces and nephews to town to visit their maternal grandparents. When the children had exhausted their hosts, Robert and Lydia took them to Green Park for a picnic in their grandparents' open carriage.

"I do not know what I would have done without you during those first terrible months," Robert said to Lydia ruefully over the bobbing heads of her little sister Aggie and his niece, Melanie, who had become fast friends and were always whispering secrets to one another.

"You would have managed very well, I promise you," Lydia said. She paused to extract Matthew from the side of the large, open carriage when he appeared to be about to tumble out of it. "It is I who am grateful to you for providing some relief from the inexpressible boredom of being waited on hand and foot by all of Alexander's irritatingly solicitous servants," she added as she deposited the squirming child on her lap.

Robert gave a bark of laughter.

"Well, you are not likely to be bored in *this* company," he said, putting an affectionate hand on Matthew's curly head.

"Here, Matthew," he added as he picked Matthew up and seated him on his own lap. "You are too heavy for Miss Whittaker." Matthew put both his arms around Robert's neck, and Robert's face softened as he hugged the child.

Lydia smiled affectionately at Robert. She did not know another man, except perhaps Alexander, who would have disrupted months of his life to devote all of his time to comforting his grieving wards.

The sad, anxious, unnaturally solemn children of last autumn had been replaced by these laughing, wriggling, mischievous little rascals.

Thank God.

The children let out a cheer as Robert's coachman guided the carriage through the gates of the park. They had been confined for an interminable quarter of an hour, and they were ready to *run*.

"Keep within our sight!" Lydia called after them as they started for the path. She was gratified to see that her sisters skidded to a halt as if pulled by invisible strings. The other children followed their example and checked their progress as well.

"You will be a wonderful mother someday," Robert said, taking a food basket in each hand.

"If I can find a man who will put up with my managing ways, I suppose I will," she said with a laugh. Her eyes narrowed and she looked on up ahead. "Amy! Take Matthew's hand, if you please! And Aggie, you take little Mary's!"

"Yes, Lydia," the nine-year-old called back as she evaded Matthew's efforts to escape from her.

Lydia's heart swelled with affection. Amy was a born mother hen. And sweet, good-natured little Aggie interrupted her confidences to Melanie to run after Mary. They remained lovable little girls despite all of Alexander's spoiling.

"No!" barked Robert with steel in his voice when his older nephew, Mark, walked up to a tree and eyed its lower branches speculatively.

Lydia burst into laughter.

"You are quite getting the hang of the thing, Robert!"

"We have been such good friends, Lydia," he said warmly. "Maybe it is time to become something more."

Lydia's eyes flew to his face. They had always been friendly, but this intimate tone of voice was something new.

"I saw Lady Madelyn. All is at an end between us."

"I am sorry, Robert," Lydia said carefully. "I know how devoted you were to her."

"I cannot ask her to share my burdens, happy ones though they are. I love my nieces and nephews. I could not send them to boarding school as Madelyn wishes."

"I should hope not," Lydia said, appalled that even Lady Madelyn would suggest such a thing.

"Madelyn is as far above my touch as an angel is above a beggar's," he said with a sigh.

"An angel, indeed!" Lydia scoffed, remembering all of Lady Madelyn's little snubs and slights.

He stopped, put the baskets on the ground, and took both of Lydia's hands in his.

"I need a wife, Lydia," he said softly.

She stared at him, uncomprehending for a moment. Then she gasped and pulled her hands away.

"You mean me?" She gave a brittle laugh. "Now *there* is gallantry for you! Lady Madelyn is too fine and delicate to share your burdens, but good old Lydia is just the thing!"

"Think, Lydia! I am hardly a pauper, and I can provide for you very well. The children like you. I like you. And you are hardly besieged by other suitors."

"How *very* tactful of you to point that out," she said dryly.

He grinned.

"There has always been truth between us, my girl. I can think of no better foundation for a successful marriage."

"What about a *happy* marriage, Robert? You love Lady Madelyn, and I love—"

She broke off in consternation, shocked that she had almost betrayed her secret to him.

"Lieutenant Edward Whittaker," Robert said softly. "My poor Lydia."

Oh, why bother denying it?

"I am 'good old Lydia' to him as well," she said bitterly. She could not bear the look of pity in his eyes. "He is as far above me as Lady Madelyn is above you."

"Then why should we not find consolation together?" he asked. "Not to puff myself up, my dear, but I am considered quite a good catch."

"The best an ape-leader like me is likely to get, you mean," she said, effortlessly reading his mind.

"You are the most *horrid* girl," he said with a grin. "No wonder I like you so much. You need not give me an answer now."

"But I will," she said, proceeding down the path. "Thank you ever so much for your *excessively* flattering offer, Robert, but I fear I must decline."

Robert merely sighed.

"Someday when you are married to a woman you love to distraction, you will look upon this day's work and *shudder,*" Lydia added cheerfully.

"I will not change my mind," he said earnestly. "If you change yours, you have only to send me word."

Lydia sat with the wallflowers and watched the gaily dressed couples dance a Scottish reel. Lady Letitia had gone to great pains to procure vouchers to Almack's for Lydia and Amelia, but it was hard to be grateful when her mind was disturbed by her fears for Edward.

"How can they *dance* at a time like this!"

Lydia had not spoken aloud, but she was in wholehearted agreement with the sentiment. She had been so occupied with her own thoughts that she did not notice Amelia had come to sit beside her.

"I know," Lydia said, patting Amelia's restless hand for comfort.

"I would have gone mad if you had not persuaded your brother-in-law to give you news from the battle before it appeared in the newspapers. I do not know how to thank you!"

"Do not regard it, I pray you," Lydia said, feeling guilty for letting Amelia believe it was for *her* sake that she'd shamelessly bullied Alexander into sharing the contents of the unofficial intelligence reports with her. "Remember, it is supposed to be a secret. Alexander could get into trouble for sharing the contents of the dispatches with civilians."

"I know. I have told no one."

"The new casualty lists are due tomorrow," Lydia said. The girls exchanged solemn glances.

Lydia had learned from Alexander that on the evening of June 18, Wellington ordered the 10th to attack the enemy cavalry at Waterloo. One squadron was lost; part of the 10th bravely charged on until they encountered a battalion of the French Old Imperial Guard. The regiment rallied under their fire and then charged, putting the Imperial Guard and its supporting cavalry to flight. It was the gallant charge of the 10th that finally decided the day.

London had gone mad with celebration, certain that the war was over.

Well, London had thought the same a year ago, Lydia thought wryly, and just *look* at what had happened. The Allied Powers had not even finished bickering over the conditions of the pact at the Congress of Vienna before Napoleon escaped and started the war up again.

Lydia would wait to rejoice when she knew Edward was safe. And Lieutenant Lowell, too, of course.

Mrs. Whittaker sat down on Lydia's other side, putting an end to the conversation between the two young ladies.

"Why are the two of you not dancing?" the elder lady demanded.

"Perhaps because no gentlemen have asked us," Lydia replied with a smile as she adjusted her mother's lace collar so it would lay down more becomingly.

"Well, stop hiding in the corner and perhaps some of them will!" Mrs. Whittaker said, making little shooing motions with her hands.

"All right, Mama," Lydia said, exchanging a droll look with Amelia. The young ladies obediently got up to take a turn around the room.

"Your Lydia is such a kind, sensible girl," Mrs. Coomb said as she seated herself beside Mrs. Whittaker.

"Yes," Mrs. Whittaker said vehemently. "I should like to shake her until her teeth rattle."

"Why would you want to do any such thing?" Mrs. Coomb asked in astonishment. "It must be a wonderful thing to have a daughter who never gives one a moment's anxiety."

"When I *have* such a daughter," Mrs. Whittaker said tartly as she watched Lydia stand like a block at the side of the room, neglecting to even *try* flirting with the very eligible widower standing close by, "I shall be sure to let you know."

The gentleman started to approach Lydia, but she merely gave him an absent smile and returned to her brooding. The gentleman walked away, and Mrs. Whittaker shook her head in disgust.

"Did you see that?" she demanded of her cousin. "It is no wonder my poor nerves are in such a state. The girl does *nothing* to attract eligible men."

"Well, that one is a bit old for her," Mrs. Coomb pointed out. "What about that nice Mr. Langtry? He seems quite attentive to Lydia. Amelia and I encountered them together yesterday when we were walking in the park."

"It will come to nothing," Mrs. Whittaker predicted glumly. "She will not make the slightest push to attach him. I keep telling her that a girl of only moderate looks and no fortune cannot afford to be too choosy, but to no avail."

"My Amelia is just as bad," Mrs. Coomb said. "With her beauty and the fortune her father settled on her, she could look as high as she wished for a husband. But it is nothing but Quentin this and Quentin that from morning until night, so I suppose I will have to allow the match in the end, even though he is a younger son."

Mrs. Whittaker made sympathetic noises, but she could hardly feel sorry for Mrs. Coomb, who had received a respectable offer for her daughter in her first season.

Amelia, she noticed, had found a partner and was dancing. Lydia, the provoking girl, was helping one of the dowagers settle herself into a chair with the cup of tea she had procured for her.

What was she to *do* with the wretched girl, Mrs. Whittaker wondered in despair.

"You are out early today, Lydia," Alexander said gravely when Lydia was ushered into the little room he used as a home office when he was staying at Stoneham House. "You will want to see these, I expect."

He handed her the casualty list, and she gratefully pounced upon it. Her anxious expression lightened a little as she paused over the Ls. But she looked up at Alexander questioningly when she got to the last page.

"I suppose you want this one, too," he said wryly as he handed her another sheet of paper.

It was the part of the list that contained the Ws, and Lydia gave a long sigh of relief when she did not find Edward's name there.

Alexander frowned when she gave the papers back.

"He was just toying with you, you know," he said.

"I suppose you, Vanessa, and all your acquaintances have

had a good laugh over dowdy old Lydia behaving like a lovesick ninny," she said tartly as heat flamed in her cheeks.

"How could you think I would do such a thing?" he asked. The kindness in his voice brought tears of humiliation to Lydia's eyes. "The bad blood between your families is enough to prevent a match between you. And you know he would be considered a great fool by society if he married a young lady whose fortune is so unequal to his. You could not expect it of him."

"You married Vanessa."

"That was different. Vanessa is—"

"Beautiful. I know."

"That is *not* why I—"

"Thank you, Alexander, for showing me these," she interrupted, indicating the papers on the desk. She felt tears start to her eyes; she cried so easily these days. "I am sorry to have disturbed you."

She blindly made her way out of Stoneham House and went home. She had intended to go at once to Amelia's house to tell her that neither Lieutenant Lowell nor Edward was on the casualty list, but she knew if she showed her red eyes and sad face to Amelia, her poor cousin would faint dead away for fear that her Quentin had been killed.

Lydia stole quietly into the house only to be met in the hall by her mother.

"There you are," Mrs. Whittaker screeched as she grabbed Lydia's arm in a grip surprisingly strong for a woman of such frail appearance. She pushed her into the parlor.

"Mother! What has happened?" Lydia cried. Mrs. Whittaker looked positively wild-eyed.

An accident to one of the girls, Lydia thought with a sinking heart. Amy and Aggie were still abed when Lydia left the house, but Mary Ann had been sent to an exclusive finishing school in Bath a short time ago.

Oh, please do not let it be Mary Ann!

"How *could* you be such a fool!" Mrs. Whittaker cried.

"Me? What have I done?" Lydia asked, startled.

"What have you done? You can ask? When I received Mrs. Langtry's letter telling me how delighted she was at the prospect of having you for a daughter-in-law, I could not believe it. Apparently Robert told her before he left Yorkshire that he was going to ask you to marry him, and Mrs. Langtry assumed—as would *any* sensible person—that you would have the intelligence to accept him!"

Lydia could only gape at her mother in dismay. It never occurred to her that Mrs. Langtry would write to her mother about Robert's intention of proposing. It probably was all over their old neighborhood in Yorkshire by now.

"Mother, I—"

"Tell me plain, Lydia," she demanded. "Did Robert ask you to marry him?"

"Yes," she admitted. "But, Mother, he is not in love with me."

"I knew it!" her mother shrieked. "You listen to me, my girl! You are going to sit down at once and write to Robert Langtry. Give him any excuse you please for being foolish enough to reject his proposal, but you are going to beg his pardon and agree to marry him!"

"Mother! I cannot do that!"

"Stubborn girl!" her mother cried, dissolving into bitter tears. "You *deserve* to be a spinster!"

"Well, I *did* warn you I am quite a catch," Robert said archly when Lydia told him about her mother's reaction to the news that she had rejected his proposal.

He took her hand to promenade with her between the lines of dancers.

"You *had* to tell your mother you were going to ask me!" she said reproachfully. "And she, of course, was so certain I would accept that she did not hesitate to write to *my* mother about it!"

"At the risk of sounding like a coxcomb, it did not occur to me, either, that you would not accept."

"Mother will make my life miserable until something else occurs to distract her. This would be a *wonderful* time for Vanessa to announce that she is going to have a child, but one can never depend on one's relatives to oblige one. I am afraid it is all over town by now that I have rejected your offer. The *last* thing I want to do is embarrass you, Robert."

They were separated by a movement of the dance. When they came together again, he smiled winsomely at her.

"If you are sincere about wishing to spare me embarrassment, you *could* reconsider and marry me after all."

Lydia gave him an impatient look.

"Robert, you know very well you do not love me."

"A gentleman who proposes marriage to a young lady might reasonably be assumed to have *some* affection for her. And a young lady who has spent so much time comforting the gentleman and his wards after their bereavement might be assumed to have some affection for *him*."

"It is not enough, and you know it."

"It would be enough for me," Robert said with a sigh. "I thank you, at any rate, for explaining why your mother kept giving me all those sympathetic looks and heart-rending sighs at the musicale last night. It was quite unnerving."

"Mother does not have a subtle bone in her body," Lydia complained.

"What is the expression? The fruit does not fall far from the tree?"

"*Very* funny," Lydia said, giving him a reluctant smile.

Madelyn entered the ballroom with the Earl of Stoneham and Lady Letitia in time to see Robert and Lydia leave the dance floor laughing at some shared joke.

"Annabelle Whittaker is the silliest woman imaginable, so I

never pay the least attention to anything she says," Lady Letitia
told her companions, "but she swears Mr. Langtry has offered
for Lydia and she has rejected him."

The earl gave his sister a reproving look.

"What utter nonsense, Letitia. I am surprised you will dignify
one of Mrs. Whittaker's fancies by repeating it."

Madelyn looked from one of them to another in disbelief.

"Mr. Langtry? To marry Lydia Whittaker? It *cannot* be true."

"Of course not. Have we not just said so?" Lady Letitia said
with a smile.

Madelyn seethed with jealousy. Her companions might not
think it likely that Robert would want to marry a dowdy little
nobody like Lydia Whittaker, but they had not seen the way she
had wormed her way into his life with her supposed concern
for his young wards. Madelyn did not doubt for a moment that
Lydia Whittaker would use those children to get herself a husband. A girl like that was capable of *anything*.

Leaving her companions without the least semblance of an
apology, Madelyn made her way to the sidelines, where Robert
had just escorted Lydia to her mother. She caught his attention
just after he turned away from the Whittakers.

"Lady Madelyn!" he exclaimed when he saw her. Her heart
melted at the way his face lit up.

"How are you, Mr. Langtry?" she asked with an arch smile.
"You have not called since you came down to London."

"I thought it best," he said lowering his voice. "We are visiting poor Eleanor's parents and—"

"But you certainly have found time to dance attendance on
Miss Whittaker."

"Madelyn, I—"

"Are you going to ask me to dance, Mr. Langtry? I shall be
very embarrassed if you do not. People are watching."

"Of course, my dear," he said, smiling at her. "I should be
delighted."

* * *

"Did you see that! Did you see that!" Mrs. Whittaker shrieked when she saw that redheaded hussy just *snatch* Robert away in front of everybody.

"Now, Mama," Vanessa said, patting her mother's arm. "Do not make a fuss."

"She has every man in London panting after her, but she must attach Robert Langtry as well!"

"Mother!" Lydia said, patting her mother's other arm. "They are only dancing."

"I warned you, missy!" Mrs. Whittaker cried, turning on Lydia with fury in her eyes. "If Lady Madelyn steals him away from you, you have only yourself to blame!"

Lydia merely sighed and wished the interminable evening would end.

FOURTEEN

Boulogne
August, 1815

Edward picked up the pen to write another draft of the letter, even though the floor surrounding the desk in his hotel room was littered with crumpled sheets of paper. Since the occupation had begun, the 10th had been quartered in comfort. Real walls, real beds, real food.

Right now, Edward would give anything if he could turn back time and be mired in the unrelenting rain of Waterloo before he had lost his best friend.

> *My dear Cousin Lydia,*
>   *This is the letter I had hoped I would never have to write.*

Edward ran a distracted hand over his face. His eyes felt like they had broken glass in them.

>   *Quentin was killed yesterday in a duel forced upon him by a French cavalry officer embittered by his country's defeat. This senseless sort of bloodshed is a daily occurrence since Napoleon's surrender. That it would happen to a fine, sensible, even-tempered man like Quentin is*

incomprehensible. Quentin made me promise soon after
we embarked for the Continent that I would see the en-
closed letter reached Miss Coomb in the event of his
death. I do not know where Miss Coomb resides, so I am
forced to entrust this sad commission to you and hope
you can find the words to comfort her. I know I cannot.

So pitifully inadequate, he thought as he ran a hand through his hair. But it would have to do if he wanted it to go out with the regiment's mail to England. He would send the two letters to Lord Blakely at his country home, which was where he was most likely to be at this season, and hope his sense of decency would force him to give them to Lydia.

He dared not address the envelope directly to Lydia for fear her mother would put it on the fire without even telling Lydia about it. It was exactly what Edward's own mother would do, after all, if a letter for him arrived from That Woman's daughter.

His letter to Lydia was too formal, the sort of thing one might write to a complete stranger. He knew better than to adopt any more intimate tone when Lord Blakely and possibly Lydia's mother might read it.

God, how he missed her! With Quentin's death, Edward had finally realized how precious life was and how quickly it could be taken away.

None of us know how much time we have left. Poor Quentin's sad history had taught him that.

His friend had refused to elope with his love because it was the honorable thing to do, and his reward was to go to war and die before he could marry her. They might have had a few weeks of happiness before he left for war. Now they would have nothing.

Well, it was too late for Quentin and Amelia, but it was *not* too late for Edward to grasp what happiness he could with Lydia.

When Edward reached England, he would convince Lydia to marry him across the anvil if he had to, and anyone who objected could go straight to perdition.

* * *

Alexander's eyebrows rose when he saw the boldly written return address on the battered envelope. Why would Lieutenant Edward Whittaker be writing to him?

Lord Blakely,
    I hope you will do me the very great favor of seeing that the enclosed letters are given to my Cousin Lydia. They concern my late friend, Lieutenant Lowell, and the commission he laid upon me to make sure the letter addressed to Miss Coomb reached her in the event of his death.

Lowell was one of the names Lydia had hoped not to find on the casualty lists she searched so faithfully. Alexander had no love for Lieutenant Whittaker, but he could sympathize with him on this occasion. Alexander had lost more than one good friend in the war.

He carefully put the letters back into the original envelope and went in search of Lydia.

Lydia's journey to Brighton, where Amelia and her mother were staying for the summer, took only one day because she bullied the driver into setting an uncomfortable pace.

Her eyes blurred when she passed the barracks where the 10th had been housed during those happy weeks the previous summer when she and Amelia walked out with the two dashing lieutenants almost daily. Now the laughing, good-natured Lieutenant Lowell was gone.

Amelia was red-eyed but composed when she stood to hug Lydia. Amelia was wearing black, just as if she were widowed. In her heart, she probably was.

"It is good of you to come, Lydia," Amelia said, giving her a brave smile.

"My poor dear," Lydia said. "I am so very sorry."

Amelia's eyes misted and she gave a determined sniff.

"Thank you, Lydia. Mother and I are leaving Brighton soon. I cannot bear the sight of the place now."

"Amelia, I have brought a letter that Lieutenant Lowell wanted you to have in the event of his death. Cousin Edward sent it to me."

"Oh, Lydia! How kind of you," Amelia exclaimed, eagerly holding out her hand for the letter. Unsure of what to do with herself, Lydia went into another room to give Amelia some privacy to read it.

"Lydia, my dear," Mrs. Coomb said in pleased surprise when she passed by the doorway and saw her. "I did not know you were coming to Brighton. Is your mother with you?"

"No. I came alone to give Amelia a letter Lieutenant Lowell wrote to her before his death. My cousin sent it to me."

Mrs. Coomb's pleasant expression tightened into one of annoyance.

"Well, Lydia," she said coldly. "I do wish you had consulted me first. How is Amelia to get over that unfortunate young man's death if people will constantly remind her of it?"

"It was his wish for Lydia to have the letter," Lydia said, taken aback. "How could I refuse to deliver it?"

"The sooner she gets over this unpleasant business the better," Mrs. Coomb declared. "How is she going to find a husband, pray, if she goes about with a lachrymose expression and refuses to look at another young man?"

"She loved him," Lydia said, knowing how she would feel if it were Edward who had died. "It may be some time before she is ready to consider marriage to another."

Mrs. Coomb sniffed.

"What do silly young girls know of love? I am taking her to London for the little season. My poor girl needs cheering up."

"I believe I will be on my way," Lydia told her, amazed that anyone could be so unfeeling.

"Yes, my dear," Mrs. Coomb agreed at once. "I think it best that do you not stay. Seeing you is certain to disturb Amelia since the four of you went around together all last summer. I wish you a safe journey home."

And at that, Lydia found herself on the other side of the door.

Edward frowned when he saw the battered letter that obviously had followed his regiment around France for several months.

It was from Mr. Kenniston. Perhaps he wanted to inform Edward that a more favorable suitor had petitioned for Lady Madelyn's hand, and he had approved the match. He hoped so.

To Edward's dismay, it was the opposite.

Mr. Kenniston was delighted to inform Edward that he had decided to approve a match between Edward and Lady Madelyn because Edward had distinguished himself in battle. Edward's name was mentioned twice in the dispatches and had appeared in the newspapers, something Edward had not known until now and could not have cared less about.

Just what Edward needed—another interfering busybody trying to orchestrate his life for him.

Edward tore the letter in half and threw it into the dustbin.

The new year found the streets of London full of soldiers celebrating their part in the victory, but still the 10th Hussars had not come home.

As soon as the papers came from London each day, Lydia disappeared with them into the library. Alexander knew she was searching them for any mention of her cousin or the 10th Hussars.

He debated with his conscience one cold but sunny afternoon when he received news from the War Department. But the anxious look on Lydia's face when he confronted her in the hall after the papers were delivered decided him.

"May I have a word with you in my office, please, Lydia?"

Lydia already had one hand on the stack of papers, and her expression was a study in reluctance. He was doing the right thing, Alexander assured himself, even though his mother-in-law would consider giving Lydia news about the son of her greatest enemy a betrayal of her trust.

"Sit down, my dear," he said. He could tell he had alarmed her. She was pale but composed. Fortunately, Lydia never had hysterics. It was what he admired most about her. But Alexander knew that her sensible manner concealed a loyal and tender heart.

Damn Edward Whittaker! If he hurt her, Alexander would *kill* him.

"You have had news," Lydia said, taking the seat across from his desk. "Is it . . . Cousin Edward?"

"I do not know yet whether there is cause for alarm," he told her gravely. "Their ship left the Continent several weeks ago, but it still has not been sighted. Even allowing for storms and other mishaps, they should have been in England by now. Perhaps I am wrong to tell you, but—"

"No! You did right," Lydia said, biting her lip. She took a deep, shuddering breath.

"Lydia, I know you have a . . . special regard for your cousin," he said carefully, "and I trust to your good sense not to—" He broke off with a self-conscious laugh. "Lord, I am making a mull of this. But I imagine you know what I mean to say."

"Certainly, Alexander," she said calmly, "for it is precisely what I told Vanessa about *you* the whole time she was searching the London papers for a glimpse of your name when you were at war."

"Touché, my dear," Alexander said wryly.

Lydia grinned at him.

"Thank you for telling me, Alexander," Lydia said as her smile faded. "I *am* grateful." She hesitated. "And Alexander—"

"Do not worry," he said, holding up one hand. "I will not tell your mother that you have been inquiring after your cousin's fate."

"Thank you," Lydia said grimly. "She has not despaired of seeing me married to Robert Langtry, I am afraid." She gave him an accusatory look. "I suppose *you* think I should accept him, too."

Alexander made a gesture of mock surrender.

"Not I! The fellow is fickle beyond permission, if you ask me. First he wanted Vanessa, then he wanted Madelyn, and now he wants you."

"Yes. His taste *does* seem to be deteriorating."

"That is not what I meant at all," Alexander said with a sigh. "And you know it perfectly well."

"I know," Lydia acknowledged with a brief smile. "You will tell me if you learn anything else about Edward's regiment, will you not?"

She looked so anxious.

"Of course," he said, patting her icy hand. "I have been thinking, Lydia, that all of us might go to London later this month when I take my seat in Parliament."

Lydia's face suddenly flushed with happiness. Of course she knew that he was offering to take her to London because there he would receive news of the missing Royal 10th Hussars more quickly.

"Alexander, you are the best of brothers-in-law," Lydia said gratefully.

They rose from their chairs, and Alexander gave Lydia a kiss on the cheek.

"I do not want to see you hurt," he said, feeling helpless.

For the first time since his wedding day, his prickly little sister-in-law gave him a hug. After all this time, Lydia finally seemed to realize that Alexander was on her side.

He only hoped he would not have to betray her trust by giving her news that would break her heart.

FIFTEEN

"When your mother finds out I have been a party to this mad escapade, she is going to give me a tongue-lashing that I will never forget," Alexander said wryly as he touched his leader lightly with the whip.

Lydia was riding on the box with him because Amelia was napping inside. She gave him a conspiratorial little smile.

"Now, Alexander. When you told me his ship had been sighted, you knew I would want to meet it. It is mostly for Amelia, anyway. It is important to her to see Edward, for she wants to find out about poor Lieutenant Lowell's last days."

Alexander gave her a quizzical look.

"You are dying to throw yourself into Edward Whittaker's manly arms, and you know it."

"Well, one can always hope," she said with a demure smile.

She looked so happy and relieved that Alexander did not have the heart to argue further.

"Do not look so worried," she told him. "You are doing the right thing, I promise you."

If only he could be sure.

* * *

Land, thank God! Edward felt his heart thud at the solid feel of *his* England beneath his feet. Never did he dream that his regiment would finally embark upon the ship for home only to almost become shipwrecked on the Goodwins.

Edward hoped he was not a superstitious man, but he had begun to wonder if he was fated to return to England at all.

He was waiting with his gear by the side of the ship for the horses to be unloaded when he heard her voice calling his name.

"Lydia?" he said, blinking into the strong sunlight. It would not surprise him if his mind was playing tricks on him.

She was running toward him, and Edward leisurely memorized every detail of this delightful vision. She was wearing a green dress and a fur-trimmed, russet-colored cloak with the hood down. Her hair was prettily tousled by the wind.

He grinned and held out his arms.

"Lydia, my sweet," he said, laughing aloud as she propelled herself into them. A moment ago he had been weary, hungry, wet, and freezing, but now he was deliriously happy. "Good Lord, you feel good."

"Cousin Edward," she said primly, but the little smile on her face told him she was pleased.

Staring at them was an enigmatic Lord Blakely and a little black-clad waif whom Edward recognized with some difficulty as Amelia Coomb. This unsmiling girl with the huge, haunted eyes was a mere ghost of her formerly pretty and vivacious self.

Edward felt as if someone had dashed a bucket of cold water over his head.

"Miss Coomb," he said, holding out his hand. The girl's lower lip trembled as she took it. Such a frail little hand, he thought as he cradled it tenderly in both of his.

"I had to come," she said huskily. "You were with Quentin when he—" She could not continue.

"You were in his thoughts every minute," Edward assured her, hoping it was the right thing to say.

"Lieutenant Whittaker!" one of the men from the boat shouted. "Your horse!"

Edward was glad that his was not one of the horses that had been washed overboard, but the timing could not have been more awkward. Lord Blakely surprised him by stepping forward and hailing the man who had called him.

"Here, I will hold the lieutenant's horse," he said. Lydia walked with him to give Edward and Miss Coomb privacy.

"Thank you for sending Quentin's letter to Lydia for me," Miss Coomb said. "It has meant so much to me to have it to read when I am missing him so much."

"I know," Edward said. "I miss him, too."

"No one seems to understand how much I loved him," she said with a sigh. "My mother thinks I can find another man and forget all about Quentin if I put my mind to it, but love is not like that, is it?"

"No, Miss Coomb," Edward said, thinking of Lydia. "It is not. I am glad you are here, for I have a favor to ask of you."

"I will do anything you wish," the girl told him, "after your kindness to Quentin and to me."

"I received a letter from Quentin's parents shortly before the regiment left for England. Every letter he wrote to them was full of you, and so they wish to meet you."

"Oh! I would be so pleased," she said eagerly. "What a comfort it would be to talk with someone who knew Quentin when he was a child."

"It would help them to talk to you, too," he said. He kissed her hand. "I had better relieve Lord Blakely of my horse. Thunder tends to get a bit snappish when he has been confined in a ship's hold for too long, especially when he almost gets washed overboard."

"I think you had better take a look at your horse's right hock," Lord Blakely called out when he saw that Edward and Miss Coomb had finished their conversation.

"Thank you, Lord Blakely. I shall certainly do that," Edward said, putting his hand on Lydia's shoulder when they approached. "Cousin Lydia—"

She looked into his eyes and the sensual lower lip that drove him mad quivered a bit.

"Lydia," he whispered, kissing her right on her surprised mouth. He wanted to nibble on that tender lip, but he thought he had better restrain himself; Lord Blakely looked as if he would cheerfully gut him with a dull knife.

"That will be enough of *that*," Lord Blakely said sternly as he took Lydia's arm and pulled her away.

"My apologies," Edward said with an unrepentant grin. "It has been a long time since I have had the opportunity to kiss a pretty girl. I could not resist."

"We must leave you now," Lord Blakely said, looking down his aristocratic nose at him.

"Lord Blakely, I am obliged to you for bringing Cousin Lydia and Miss Coomb to welcome me home."

"Not at all," His Lordship said, favoring Edward with an insincere smile. "I am pleased to see you returned safely."

In a pig's eye. You wish me to the devil.

"Thank you," Edward said.

"Come along, ladies," Lord Blakely said as he took Miss Coomb's arm and gave a jerk of his head to indicate that Lydia was to precede them.

She looked back at Edward with an expression that told him her whole heart.

She loves me, he thought, rejoicing inwardly. *Now all I have to do is figure out how to convince her to defy everyone* else *she loves to marry me.*

The smugglers.

Edward had forgotten all about the bloody smugglers.

To his disgust, he and the other members of the regiment were immediately posted off to Hastings and then Worthing to chase smugglers, when what he really wished to do was work on the far more attractive problem of convincing Lydia to marry him.

Fortunately, the squadron under his command and three others from the 10th were selected to serve on review duty in London in March. With luck he could manage to see Lydia before they posted him off somewhere else.

The city would still be a bit thin of company before the official start of the season, but Lord Blakely's political career would have kept him in London. Perhaps Lydia and her family remained with him.

The day after Edward returned to London, he and the members of his squadron were riding down St. James on the way to make an appearance at court when he spotted Lydia herding a group of four little girls along the street. He could not resist straightening in his saddle and rapping out a sharp command to his men. The last time Lydia saw him, he had been unkempt and weary. He wanted to impress her.

He knew when Lydia spotted him, for she jerked as if an imaginary string tied to her body had been pulled tight. Eyes wide, she stared right at him until the children began demanding attention. Lydia pointed to the soldiers and made some comment.

She looked so pretty in her matching blue pelisse and bonnet. It took all the discipline Edward possessed not to leap off his horse and sweep her into his arms.

He had to laugh at himself for thrusting his chest out a little farther and sucking his stomach in. He wondered with uncharacteristic vanity what his love was saying to her young charges.

She would say, there is my cousin, Edward Whittaker, member of the Prince of Wales's Own Royal 10th Hussars.

"Stay away from the street," Lydia told the children. "Even highly bred, well-disciplined horses can be shockingly unpredictable in their personal habits."

Just like men, she added to herself.

She had recognized Edward at once, of course. Her silly heart swelled with love at the mere sight of him. All during the rest of January she had hoped for a glimpse of him, but she had searched in vain along the street and at every party she attended. Her new preoccupation with her appearance quite delighted her mother and long-suffering maid.

After a while Lydia had assumed the 10th was doing peacekeeping duty somewhere along the coast. Edward had kissed her so warmly in January. Could he have forgotten her existence already?

Today, of course, when she finally saw him, she was wearing an old blue pelisse and bonnet because she was escorting her sisters and Robert's two nieces to town to buy new shoes.

Not that it mattered. He probably did not notice her among the other pedestrians.

He is in London, she thought, despairing. *He is right here in London, and he has made no attempt whatsoever to see me.*

It was just as he had joked; Lydia was merely a convenient female pair of lips when the war hero had need of them.

"Come along, girls," she said briskly, shooing her menagerie of giggling moppets ahead of her. Keeping the lively children from rolling under some sportsman's carriage wheels, thank heavens, was a useful distraction when one's dearest hopes have been dashed.

"It is quite a settled thing, my dear," Lady Letitia told Annabelle Whittaker in one of her few affable moments. It was unusual for her to make Mrs. Whittaker her confidante, and Annabelle was vastly flattered that Lady Letitia joined them in the parlor when they had come to see Vanessa. "Mr. Kenniston has withdrawn his objections to Lieutenant Whittaker as a husband for Madelyn."

Mrs. Whittaker sniffed. "I find it hard to believe good of anyone who is the son of Henry Whittaker and That Woman."

"But Lieutenant Whittaker is a fine figure of a man," Lady Letitia said benevolently. "He will come into a fortune when his father and grandfather die, and he distinguished himself for valor in the late war, you know. Mr. Kenniston was quite impressed."

Mrs. Whittaker glanced over to the corner of the room where Lydia was sitting, as still as death, looking at her hands. The provoking girl was positively bumptious in company.

"Personally, this could not come at a better time," Lady Letitia said. "We were afraid that Madelyn would attach herself to that neighbor of yours. What was his name?"

"Mr. Langtry," Lydia said from her corner of the room.

"Mr. Langtry," Lady Letitia acknowledged with a little nod, "is quite a good sort of man and might do very well for an undistinguished miss, but he is hardly a suitable match for a young lady as beautiful, accomplished, and wealthy as Madelyn."

Since Mrs. Whittaker had told Lady Letitia herself that Robert Langtry had proposed to Lydia, one could hardly acquit her of malicious intent. However, Letitia's shaft fell far short of its mark because Mrs. Whittaker knew perfectly well the gentleman would not have chosen Lydia if he had not been left with his brother's children to rear.

All the more reason for Lydia to accept him.

So Edward was to marry Lady Madelyn.

How suitable.

What a fool Lydia had been to think it could be otherwise.

Lydia managed to excuse herself and get to her room before the tears started running down her cheeks. She took her grandmother's amethyst ring from her dresser drawer and held it in her palm. She had sustained herself during the long months of waiting for news of Edward by trying it on her finger and pretending that he had placed it there out of tenderness and love.

But he was going to marry Lady Madelyn. It was quite a settled thing, according to Lady Letitia. Lydia would have to give the ring back to Edward the next time she saw him so he could give it to *her*.

It was raining, a perfect day to suit her mood. Lydia put on her old bonnet and pelisse, and decided to go to the library. Alexander had very kindly treated her to a subscription, or she would have gone mad during the long months of waiting to hear Edward's fate.

"You went to the library yesterday," Amy pointed out when Lydia asked if the girls would like to accompany her.

"I know. I already read the book I borrowed yesterday, and I need another," Lydia said. "You do not have to go if you do not want to."

"*I* want to go!" Aggie cried, afraid Lydia would rescind the invitation.

"Mama does not like it when you wear that old bonnet in public," Amy warned her older sister.

"I am not about to ruin a new bonnet in the rain," Lydia said. "Are you going to tell on me?"

"No," Amy said, shocked.

"May we stop for peppermints?" Aggie asked hopefully.

Lydia had to smile in spite of her broken heart.

"I think so," she said, "*if* you promise to be good girls for Miss Crump and do your lessons without complaint when we come back."

"Yes, Lydia," the girls chorused.

As Lydia and her sisters made their way up the street, the rain got worse and she was glad she wore her old bonnet. She was also glad her mother could not see her with her hair scraggling in the rain and her pelisse damp and looking bedraggled.

The girls kept squealing when they got splashed by passing

carriages, but Lydia assumed they were having a good time because they objected when she suggested turning back.

Lydia was not the only one looking for a book to while away the bad weather, for the library was fairly crowded. She settled the girls on a bench and went off in search of a book. She decided that this was not the day to try to improve the tone of her mind, and perused the row of sensational novels from Minerva Press. She had just picked up what she hoped would be the most lurid among them when a familiar male voice chuckled in her ear.

She spun around and found herself in Edward's loose embrace.

"Well met, Cousin Lydia. I have been wanting to talk to you."

"I know. I should have given it back to you at once when you returned safe to England, but I—" *could not have remembered my own name when you kissed me that day at the dock.* Lydia backed up against the shelf to give herself distance from him. He advanced and put his hands on the racks above her head so she had to bend backward to look up into his face. She could not *breathe* when he was standing so close. "I do not have it with me," she said, "but I will give it back as soon as I can."

Edward frowned and moved his hands to her shoulders.

"I am sorry," Lydia babbled on. "I know you will be wanting the ring back so you can give it to Lady Madelyn."

"Why would I—"

"Lydia, may we—" Amy began. She and Aggie stood at the end of the shelf with wide eyes at the sight of their sister practically in the embrace of a gentleman.

Edward smiled at the girls.

"Good morning," he said.

"Good morning," the girls chorused.

"Are you going to perform the introductions, cousin?" he asked Lydia.

"Cousin Edward," Lydia said, seeing no help for it. She knew there would be trouble if they told their mother that Lydia had introduced them to the son of That Woman, but she refused to confuse the girls by asking them to conceal information. "May I present my sisters, Amy and Agatha. Girls, this is Cousin Edward. He is a lieutenant in the 10th Hussars and we saw his regiment the other day in St. James Street."

The girls performed quite creditable little bows.

"Charmed," he said, smiling.

"You are the gentleman who came to call two days ago," Aggie blurted out.

Amy gave her a severe look.

"We promised Mama we would not tell anyone," Amy said, looking guilty when Lydia bent an astonished look on her little sisters.

So much for having principles.

"Yes," Cousin Edward acknowledged. "You and your mother were not at home to callers, I believe."

"No, Mama was home," Aggie said helpfully before Amy could shush her.

Edward had called to ask for his ring back, and Lydia's mother had denied him. Lydia felt ready to sink.

"Cousin Edward, I do not know what to say to you," she said helplessly. "If I had known—"

"Say nothing, then," he interrupted as he continued to smile at the younger girls.

"Lydia," Aggie said, looking anxious. "Does this mean we may not have the peppermints?"

"No. Of course not," she said, grateful to the child for giving her the excuse she needed to end this awkwardness. "Cousin Edward, we must be on our way. It will soon be time for their lessons, and I did promise them I would buy them some peppermints before we returned home."

Edward stepped smoothly between the two little girls and offered his arms, just as if they were grown ladies and he was their escort. He winked at Lydia.

"I do not see a single book I wish to read, so if you do not object I should like to accompany you," he said.

The girls beamed.

"Are you really our cousin?" Amy asked.

"Certainly," he said. "Your father was my uncle."

"You are horrid Uncle Henry's son," Amy said importantly.

"Er, yes," Edward said, trying not to laugh. Lydia was going to crawl into a hole, just as soon as she found one. She could hardly scold Amy when she had called her uncle by the nickname often in the child's hearing.

"Alexander says the soldiers in the blue uniforms are just toy soldiers," Aggie said, eager to prove she was not the only one with inside knowledge.

"Aggie!" Lydia exclaimed, absolutely horrified. Alexander had often remarked that in his days with the 10th Hussars in 1812, he had done little except ride down the streets of Brighton in his splendid blue uniform and attend a great many balls. But since that time the regiment had distinguished itself in battle, first in the Peninsula and then at Waterloo.

"Perhaps he was referring to our horses," Edward said pleasantly. "They are light, very swift horses that are deadly to the enemy in a cavalry charge. They are somewhat small, and for that reason none of us can be over a certain height and weight. Lord Blakely was quite the military man himself, I am told."

"Alexander was a hero," Amy said. "But now he has to stop being a hero because he is married to our sister."

"Here is the shop," Lydia announced with some relief.

"So it is," Edward murmured, ushering his companions inside and buying each of them a large peppermint stick. Lydia tried to demur when he handed one to her.

"Lydia is not supposed to have sweets because they make her fat," Aggie explained helpfully.

"Aggie!" Lydia said with a despairing sigh.

"Well, that is what Mama says."

"That was a long time ago," Lydia said.

"Yes, Aggie," Amy said reprovingly. "It has been ever so long since Lydia burst the seams in her carriage dress."

"Ah. So there can be no objection now," Edward said, intervening smoothly, quite possibly saving Amy's life. He proffered the candy and Lydia took it, hoping that this would keep her sisters from confiding any other secrets to Edward.

He walked them almost to their door.

"I should like to have a word with your sister, if you please," he said to the little girls.

"Good-bye, Cousin Edward," Amy said politely as the two girls bowed.

"Thank you for the peppermint sticks," Aggie added.

Then they scurried inside, no doubt to inform the entire household that they had met their Cousin Edward, the toy soldier.

"Delightful girls," Edward said to Lydia as he drew her behind a large tree across the street from the house.

"Cousin Edward, I wish to apologize—"

But she lost her train of thought as Edward backed her against the tree and tipped her chin up so he could look directly into her eyes.

"Now, my girl," he said in a whisper. "Tell Cousin Edward why you are so troubled."

He meant it kindly, of course. How was he to know that she had been stupid enough to fall in love with him? She did not know what she could say without making a fool of herself. She was almost relieved when she heard her mother's voice calling to her.

"Lydia! Where are you? Come inside the house this instant!"

Edward tried to keep Lydia hidden, but she gave him a rueful smile and extricated herself from his loose embrace.

"I am here, Mother," Lydia said, stepping out from behind the tree.

Her mother's hands were on her hips, and her voice was pure

fishwife. Lydia knew the girls probably had told her all about their meeting with their magnificent cousin.

"Good-bye, Edward," she whispered to her cousin.

Still hidden from Mrs. Whittaker, he took Lydia's hand and kissed it.

"Are you for Stoneham House tonight?" he asked.

"Yes."

"I will see you there, then," he said, giving her a speaking look.

Of course. He wanted his ring back.

SIXTEEN

When Robert received a card of invitation to a ball at Stoneham House, he could not resist attending even though he had resolved never to see Madelyn again. He supposed he was invited because he was considered Lydia's official suitor by her mother and Vanessa, if not by Lydia herself.

He had to see Madelyn just once more, even though Madelyn had made her loathing for him abundantly clear now that he had offered for Lydia.

Lady Letitia's eyes turned frosty when she saw him in the receiving line.

"Mr. Langtry," she said coolly.

Madelyn's head swiveled to face him from her place farther down in the line.

"I told you I never wanted to see you again as long as I live," she hissed when he stood before her. There was a social smile on her face, but pure fury in her magnificent green eyes.

"Madelyn, I—"

"Good evening, Lord Willoughby," she said brightly to the next person in line so that Robert would have to move on.

"And Lieutenant Whittaker! At last!" she exclaimed, even more brightly. "I know I need not stand on ceremony with you any longer, sir, so I shall depend upon you for the first set."

"Uh, charmed," the fellow said, as he took the gloved hand that Madelyn offered him and raised it to his lips.

Robert could have cheerfully murdered Whittaker for the way Madelyn was smiling at him.

He was seething with jealousy, even though he had no right. No right at all.

Lydia anticipated the ball at Stoneham House with unalloyed misery. She permitted her ecstatic maid to give vent to the full range of her talents and dress Lydia in a magnificent green satin and ivory tulle gown with a complicated arrangement of white roses and green ivy in her upswept hair. Ordinarily Lydia would have objected to sitting still while the maid wrought this tedious magic, but tonight she was too depressed to argue.

The amethyst ring was on her finger, hidden safely under her glove. As soon as she saw Edward, she would remove it and give it back to him.

A piece of her heart would go with it.

"You are awfully quiet tonight, Lydia," whispered Vanessa when she met her at Stoneham House. "You are not ill, I hope?"

"I have much to think about," Lydia replied.

"Robert's proposal, I suppose," Vanessa said. "You could do worse, but do not accept him unless you believe you can love him."

Lydia regarded her sister with astonishment.

"What? You mean you are not going to try to convince me to marry him? Are you certain *you* are not feeling ill?"

"After being married to my darling Alexander, I can only wish for you to have the same happiness. Do not marry where you cannot love."

"Thank you, Vanessa. It is refreshing not to be reminded that a woman with my plain looks had better snatch at the first opportunity she is given."

Vanessa was shocked.

"Surely Mama did not say so!"

"Of course she did. And she is not the only one, although

most of them did not state the matter quite so bluntly. Love matches are not for women of moderate looks and no accomplishments."

"No accomplishments! What a dreadful thing to say," Vanessa said fiercely. "The property in Yorkshire would have fallen down around our ears if it had not been for you. Heaven knows what we would have been reduced to eating. And wearing."

"I am afraid such mundane skills are hardly as useful to a young lady as speaking fluent Italian and playing the pianoforte."

"What utter rubbish!" Vanessa exclaimed. She was almost to the receiving line so she hastily rearranged her face into a smile. "Lady Letitia, how lovely you look! Madelyn! So pleased!"

Lydia regarded Lady Madelyn with an inward sigh. As luck would have it, they were both wearing green gowns of a similar style with short capped sleeves and tulle overskirts. Of course, Lady Madelyn's was a perfect foil for her glorious red hair. Lydia could only look like a pale imitation of her.

"Miss Whittaker," Lady Madelyn said archly as she looked Lydia up and down. "I see we share similar tastes in many things."

"So it appears," Lydia said in the same tone. No doubt she and Edward had laughed together at the pretensions of the dowdy creature who had the effrontery to fall in love with the dashing lieutenant. Or, at least, Madelyn would have laughed.

Edward would never laugh at her. He was too kind. Too perfect. Lydia could not bear to see him again; she would *die* if she could not see him again.

Do not marry where you cannot love.

Easy enough for Vanessa to say.

"Good evening, Lydia," said Robert at her elbow. Lydia jumped. She had not seen him approach.

"Mr. Langtry, I am surprised to see you. I thought you were taking the children into the country."

"There was a change in plan."

Lydia peered at him through narrowed eyes.

"What is wrong with you?"

She took a step back when Robert gave her a smile that could only be described as fierce.

"Nothing, my dear. Nothing at all."

He glanced at the reception line, made eye contact with Madelyn, and leisurely kissed Lydia's hand.

"See here! What are you about?" Lydia said, far from gratified.

"That busybody Lady Letitia told Madelyn that I offered for you."

"Did she also tell her that I refused you?"

"Yes, but she is angry just the same." He looked up, and his eyes narrowed menacingly. "Here comes that fellow now!"

"Cousin Lydia," Edward said, bowing. "May I have the second set of dances with you? Evening, Mr. Langtry."

"Certainly, Cousin Edward," she said, feeling sudden heat burn her cheeks. "I should be pleased."

He bowed.

"I shall look forward to it," he said with a smile. "If you will excuse me." He nodded to Robert and went to Lady Madelyn's side.

Robert let out a hiss of breath when Edward offered his arm and Lady Madelyn accepted it, looking up at him through her eyelashes as he led her away to the dance floor.

"Come along, Lydia," Robert said abruptly, and practically dragged Lydia to the dance floor.

Lydia sighed. She could see it was going to be a *wonderful* evening.

Edward felt as if he were on a stage and no one had given him his lines.

Lady Madelyn's languishing looks completely confounded him. She always had been perfectly polite but held him at arm's

length. Now she was hanging all over him. Of course, he had
recognized her at once as being one of the most determined
flirts of his acquaintance, but only in the most subtle and lady-
like way.

There was nothing subtle about the way she was acting tonight.

He glanced over at an adjacent circle where Lydia and Robert
were dancing.

"She dances like a sack of potatoes," Madelyn sniffed when
she saw the direction of his gaze.

"I see nothing amiss," Edward said stiffly.

"Of course not. Men are so blessedly oblivious of such re-
finements. You should hear her performance on the pianoforte.
Absolutely abysmal."

"My cousin is a very kind and capable young woman," Edward said, regretting that he could not use stronger words. "I
hold her in the highest esteem."

"I am sick to death of hearing how *worthy* the wretched creature is," Madelyn said with so much venom in her voice that
Edward stared at her.

Realizing that she had made a *gaffe,* Madelyn made a swift
recovery.

"Your loyalty to your cousin does you credit, Edward. I may
call you Edward, may I not?" That arch tone again. "It seems
ridiculous to stand on ceremony under the circumstances."

Circumstances?

"As you wish, Lady Madelyn," he said politely but cautiously.

She gave him a little *moue* of reproof.

"You must call me Madelyn," she said coyly.

"Madelyn," he repeated obediently.

To his relief, the dance was just ending. He could not wait
to relinquish her to someone else.

Langtry had finished dancing with Lydia, and left her in the
middle of the floor while he walked in their direction. Edward

was happy to see him come, for once. Edward would hand Madelyn off to him and join Lydia. But Madelyn quickly foiled this admirable plan.

"Edward, it is so stuffy in here," she said in a die-away voice. Edward looked at her in surprise. She *was* flushed.

"I shall procure a glass of punch for you," he said at once. It would serve his purpose very well, for he could collect Lydia on his way.

"No, no!" she exclaimed, attaching her slim fingers with surprising strength to his arm. "I need fresh air. Walk with me onto the balcony."

Edward flinched a little at the look in Langtry's eyes as he approached, but Madelyn left him no choice except to do as she commanded. He favored Langtry with an apologetic little shrug as he escorted Madelyn to the balcony. He was exceedingly grateful that looks could not kill.

Once in the muted darkness of the balcony overlooking Stoneham House's celebrated gardens, Edward was shocked to find Madelyn in his arms. When he tried to extricate himself from her grip, she held on all the tighter.

"I feel a little faint," she said huskily.

Edward did not believe it for a moment.

"Madelyn, what is all this about?" he snapped with some asperity.

To his dismay she burst into tears and, with a sob, buried her face in his chest.

Edward looked around helplessly, hoping there were no witnesses to this uncomfortable scene. He felt sorry for Madelyn's distress, but all he needed was for Lydia to learn that he was disporting himself with Madelyn on the balcony.

"He asked her to marry him! My godmother had it from her mother, so it must be true," she sobbed. "But he loves me. Me!"

Ah. That explained it. Langtry had offended the goddess's pride by casting his gaze elsewhere.

"I am sorry you are distressed, my dear," he said soothingly.

"If his brother had not died and saddled him with all those dreadful children, he would not look twice at her."

Edward took his handkerchief from his pocket and gave it to her. Then a horrible suspicion crossed his mind.

He closed his eyes.

"Who is this woman he is going to marry?" he asked, afraid to hear the answer.

"Lydia Whittaker."

"Has she accepted him?" Edward demanded. He gave Madelyn a little shake. "Has she?"

Wide-eyed, Madelyn stared at him.

"I imagine not yet, because there has been no formal announcement in the newspapers. But she will." Madelyn gave a brittle little laugh. "It is the best match the insignificant little mouse could hope for, and she is a fool if she does not know it."

"But—"

"I do not want to talk about *her*," Madelyn declared. She looped her arms around Edward's neck.

"What the devil!" Edward tried to unlock her arms and set her away from him. She clung like a burr.

"My guardian has withdrawn his objection to a match between us," she said.

"Madelyn, you are a very good sort of girl, but I am not going to marry you," Edward said firmly. "You know perfectly well that you do not love me."

"Well," she said, pouting. "I must marry *someone*."

"Anyone you choose, so long as it is not I."

"You are ungallant, sir!" she exclaimed indignantly.

"Excessively," he agreed. "You would be very much better off without me."

"She is going to marry him. She told me so herself," Robert told Lydia while they were waltzing.

Edward had not come to claim his dance, so Lydia could

think of no excuse for refusing to dance with Robert again. She did not enjoy being propelled about the floor by an exceedingly angry young man who was threatening all sorts of dire reprisals against the man she loved.

"Then it must be true," Lydia said in a small, defeated voice. This only confirmed her certainty that Edward wanted to speak with her so he could claim the heirloom ring for his fiancée. The band burned against her skin.

Edward would be genuinely sorry if he knew how much his marriage to Madelyn would hurt her. She knew he would be gentle and kind. It would be absolutely humiliating. Lydia could not bear Edward's pity.

"There they are," Robert said with a sneer in his voice.

Through the tears gathering in her eyes, Lydia saw Edward escort Madelyn back into the room. He looked around swiftly and made eye contact with her. His face was so grim that Lydia's heart sank.

It sank even further when he took Madelyn in his arms and led her into the whirling dancers.

He had forgotten all about his dance with Lydia because he was with Madelyn.

And what man would not?

Madelyn was everything Lydia would never be. It was time she stopped fooling herself.

"I will marry you, Robert, if you wish," Lydia whispered.

"Lydia!" he exclaimed. He pulled himself together with an effort. "I am delighted, of course."

He looked anything but delighted, but Lydia knew he was too much the gentleman to back out now. She could not love him, but she could help him rear his poor brother's children and run the two estates. She would do it to the best of her ability, she vowed.

The dance ended at that moment, and Robert kissed her hand.

"I will just have a word with Lord Stoneham," he said. "The announcement is long overdue." He strode purposefully away, and Lydia, already having second thoughts, would have followed if Edward had not caught her arm.

"Lydia, I must speak with you," he said urgently.

"Yes, Cousin Edward, I know," she said, extricating herself and removing her glove. "You will want this back for Lady Madelyn."

Her voice was husky with the effort of trying not to cry. She covered her distress with a bright smile.

"I wish you happy, Edward," she said softly, putting the ring in the palm of his hand.

"Lydia, I—"

Lord Stoneham called for order.

"Ladies and gentlemen," he said jovially. "It is my pleasure to announce that Miss Lydia Whittaker, the sister of my dear daughter-in-law, has consented to marry Mr. Robert Langtry."

The guests erupted into applause and shouts of congratulations to Robert, who walked up to Lydia and took her hand.

The orchestra struck up another waltz and Robert smoothly guided Lydia into it. Lydia glanced back into Edward's thunderstruck face.

"You will not be sorry," Robert promised her.

I already am, she thought.

Lydia woke up the next day with a headache.

"You are never ill," said Mrs. Whittaker, torn between concern and annoyance. "This cannot come at a worse time. We are promised to Robert Langtry's mother for a dinner party in your honor tonight, and one does not wish to be backward in any attention to one's future in-laws."

"I am not ill. Merely tired," Lydia said. "I will be myself by tonight."

Lydia skulked in her room all morning and did feel better by afternoon. Callers would be arriving, Lydia knew. She could not bear their congratulations and the usual gossip they would bring.

All she could think of was the look on Cousin Edward's face when Lord Stoneham made the announcement. He had not been pleased or relieved. He had been horrified.

Well, it was too late to worry about that now.

It would not have worked out between herself and Edward, Lydia told her poor, breaking heart. Their families would have torn them apart before the wedding cake was gone stale.

With Robert she would be the mistress of her own establishment. She would have those sweet children to raise, and there was the possibility of having her own children someday. The match would meet with the approval of her mother and his, and so their marriage would not be plagued by the acrimony of hostile relatives.

It would be enough.

It would *have* to be enough.

Lydia could find only so much diversion in the struggles of her spineless Minerva Press heroine in the arms of the dastardly villain, so she decided to take the book back and get another. It was not quite the thing for a young lady to go on such an excursion alone, but she could not bear company today. In keeping with her mood, she put on her old blue pelisse and bonnet. Then she stole out of the house and walked to the library.

"Miss Whittaker! I heard your excellent news. May I wish you happy?" said an acquaintance as Lydia perused the shelves of books.

"You may, I thank you," she said, summoning a smile to her face with some difficulty.

"Quite exciting," said another young lady jovially.

"My mother is delighted, of course," Lydia said, feeling like a hypocrite. "We have known the Langtrys forever."

One little cat could not resist digging in her claws.

"Such a handsome man," she said coyly. "And with all those *darling* children left on his hands for you to care for."

Naturally the mousy Miss Whittaker could not get a man otherwise.

Lydia was about to excuse herself to go back into the stacks to escape from all this goodwill when Edward walked in. In cowardly fashion, Lydia scurried to the back of the library where the less popular books were kept.

"I did not know you were interested in the Greek tragedians, Lydia," Edward said dryly as he took her by the shoulders and propped her against the wall.

Lydia was grateful, in a way. Her knees were shaking.

"You cannot marry him, you know," he said softly as he began kissing the angle of her jaw and set a burning path to her mouth. "He will make you miserable."

She knew it.

She knew it now, when it was too late.

But she did not protest. She could not, with his lips on her skin. When he took her mouth, her neck arched back to give him access as if she did this sort of thing all the time. She thought her heart would burst.

"You must not marry him," he whispered after they had broken apart. Lydia was trying very hard not to gasp for breath like an abandoned hussy.

"Robert Langtry *needs* me!" she protested.

"I need you!" Edward kissed her until her knees went weak again.

"No! Marrying me will estrange you from your parents and your grandfather and ruin your career—"

"Do you know any army wives? They are resourceful, intelligent, sensible women like *you,* Lydia. You are *perfect* for me. If my parents *do* cut me off without a shilling, you are probably the only woman I know who can contrive to keep us alive on an officer's pay."

"But you are going into the diplomatic service—"

"Will you stop quoting my mother at me? That is *her* desire, not mine. And even if I do gratify her by going into the diplomatic service, you will be an asset to me there as well."

"But Lady Madelyn—"

"Hang Lady Madelyn!" He shook her again, hard. "Do you think I do not know what you are doing? You are assessing the situation with that frighteningly logical mind of yours and deciding what role Lydia Whittaker can take to arrange everyone's lives to her satisfaction. Robert Langtry needs a nursemaid and housekeeper, so you have decided in your infinite wisdom to sacrifice your happiness for his. *I* need an accomplished social hostess who will meet the approval of my parents to unlock the floodgates of my fortune, so I must marry Lady Madelyn."

"You *cannot* want to marry me," Lydia protested.

"Kindly do me the very great favor of allowing me to know my own mind," he said, his eyes flashing. "Lydia, one of the things I admire most about you is your willingness to do for others. But at some point you must consider what is best for *yourself.*"

"And that is *you,* I suppose!"

Edward offended her mightily by bursting into reluctant laughter.

"Look at you," he said in answer to her look of indignation. "Hands on your hips. Chin thrust out to take on the world." He grabbed her again and gave her a quick kiss on the mouth. "God, I love you."

"Edward—" said Lydia, near tears.

"I will always love you," he whispered. "Lydia, you cannot marry him." Then he left her.

That night she lay awake a long time after the household was asleep.

He loved her.

Edward loved her.

She rolled over and buried her face in her pillow.

And she had ruined everything by accepting Robert.

SEVENTEEN

With a heart as heavy as lead, Lydia let her maid wind pink rosebuds through her hair and apply a delicate touch of rouge to her cheekbones. If Lydia did not feel like a happy bride, Monique would make sure she at least looked like one.

Her dress was a divine column of pink and crystal spangles that showed a great deal more of Lydia's bosom than she would have ordinarily thought decent. But she did not remonstrate when Monique refused to use the gossamer thin fichu Lydia had purchased to fill in the neckline.

What did it matter?

She was going to marry Robert. And tonight, at the ball his mother was giving in her honor at poor Eleanor and John's town house, she was going to have to pretend to be happy about it.

"Lovely!" her mother said from the doorway. "Perfectly lovely! Lydia, you have never looked so well."

"Thank you, Mother," Lydia said, trying to smile. Mrs. Whittaker had been in a state of high glee ever since the announcement.

"And I think I am not the only admirer," Mrs. Whittaker said coyly as she stood aside to let all the children stream into the room. "Here she is, darlings, your new mother."

Robert's nieces and nephews as well as her own little sisters stood around her, laughing and touching the crystal beads on her dress.

"It is beautiful," Aggie said, her eyes shining. "And Melanie is going to be my sister forever and ever."

Lydia only smiled, declining to explain the reality of relatives by marriage to her little sister.

"And you are going to be my mama," said Matthew, tugging on Lydia's skirt to get her attention. Her heart melted when she looked down into his innocent face. She kissed the top of his head, enjoying the baby warmth of his blond hair on her lips.

"Yes, Matthew," she said, smiling through sudden tears.

Monique threw up her hands in dismay.

"Tears of happiness are all very well, miss," the maid scolded, "but not when I have just applied the rouge!"

It was a nightmare.

An absolute nightmare.

To make her mood complete, the ball was being held in the late John and Eleanor Langtry's town house, which now belonged to Robert in trust for his oldest nephew and continued to contain sad memories for all of them. Having no town house of her own, it made sense for Mrs. Langtry to make use of it for this occasion.

Lydia moved through the overheated room on Robert's arm, accepting the good wishes of his mother's guests with a smile to keep from screaming at the top of her lungs.

It was the largest room in the town house, the same one that Robert's brother and sister-in-law had been laid out in.

She felt a little like a corpse herself with her face painted, the scent of roses surrounding her, and the rigidity of the corset demanded by the smooth line of her gown threatening to cut off her breath.

Lord Stoneham and Lady Letitia had been invited as connections of her sisters. And because one could not exclude their houseguest, Lady Madelyn came, too.

"Come along, my dear," Robert said to Lydia. "It is time for us to open the ball."

Lydia should have felt self-conscious in the place of honor at the head of all the dancers, but she only felt numb as she curtsied to Robert and went through the first movements of the dance. She no longer had to mind the steps with her full attention, which was unfortunate because this left her mind free to contemplate her doom.

A date three months hence had been set. It had been announced in the newspapers that morning. There could be no escape, she thought in despair, without causing a dreadful scandal.

When the dance was over, Alexander came to her side. Robert relinquished Lydia with a smile and left them. He made a wide detour around the area where Lady Madelyn was holding court over a group of infatuated male admirers. Lydia could hear her bright, artificial laugh quite clearly.

"Come along, Lydia," Alexander said, guiding her to one of the sets. "I cannot miss my opportunity to dance with the belle of the ball."

Lydia rolled her eyes.

"Hardly," she scoffed.

They parted ways to circle with the dancers of their respective genders, and when they met again Alexander looked troubled.

"Lydia, are you certain you wish to marry him?"

"This is a fine time to ask," she replied, trying to pass off the uncomfortable subject with a laugh.

"Yes," Alexander said with a smile just as unconvincing as her own. "I want so much for you to be happy."

"Happy," she mused, trying to convince herself. "I have as much chance of being happy as anyone in marriage, I suppose. Robert is a good man, and I have known him all my life. The children are darlings, and they need me. Heaven knows I shall not be bored with two households to manage."

The dance separated them again, and she met him with a determined smile when they came back together.

"And it is very pleasant to be engaged to a man who meets with the approval of my mother and all my well-wishers. You probably feared I would be left on your hands forever."

"Lydia," he said, looking pained.

When the dance was ended, Alexander started to escort her to her mother and would have walked right by Edward if he had not pointedly stood in their way.

"I trust I may have a dance with the bride," Edward said, holding out his arm for Lydia in an imperious gesture.

Alexander rose to his full height and looked menacing.

"*No,* Alexander," Lydia said under her breath as she placed her hand on Edward's arm.

Alexander relinquished Lydia, but he gave Edward a look that should have struck terror in his heart.

"I will be watching," he said to the other man.

The next dance was a waltz, but after only a few turns around the floor Edward whisked Lydia into an empty room. Lydia could not help noting it was the same room in which the funeral dinner had been laid.

"Lydia, you cannot marry him."

"I can. I *must,*" she said miserably. She could feel the tears coursing down her cheeks, but she could not stop them.

"I want you to take this." He removed the amethyst ring from his smallest finger and forced it onto her right hand.

"No! I cannot," she said in horror. "It should go to your wife."

"In my heart, *you* are my wife," he said. When she opened her mouth, he gave her a fierce look. "And if you dare to mention Lady Madelyn's name to me, I shall box your ears."

"You will forget me," she said, certain that it could not be otherwise.

"Never," he vowed, looking deeply into her eyes and kissing her fingers. "Never as long as I shall live."

A shadow fell over them, and Lydia gasped.

"It shall not be long," Alexander said quietly. "You and yours have caused enough mischief, Lieutenant Whittaker."

He stripped off his glove and drew back to strike Edward's face with it according to tradition.

"Oh, I say!" exclaimed Edward, ducking to avoid it. "Do try not to be more of an idiot than you can help, Lord Blakely. I am *not* going to meet you."

"You refuse?" Alexander said incredulously.

"Of course I refuse," he said disdainfully.

"Of course he refuses," Lydia said at the same time. "Alexander, what are you thinking of?"

"He has made you cry, and I will not stand for it."

Lydia faced Alexander with her shoulders back and her chin thrust out.

"You will not stand for it?" she scoffed. "If you think it would give me the slightest satisfaction to have you and Edward fight a duel over anything so silly, you are *much* mistaken."

"Bravo, Lydia," Edward said approvingly. "See why I love you?"

"God, Lydia," Alexander said in disgust. "And I used to have such a high opinion of your mind."

He stomped out of the room in high dudgeon.

"Edward, I cannot stay in here with you," Lydia said, feeling fresh tears well in her eyes.

How could she have been so blind? Edward loved her. He said so, and from the way he looked at her she knew it was true.

"I know, love. I know," he said, kissing her hand again. "I have made you unhappy, and I would not cause you pain for the world."

Lydia took the arm he offered and allowed him to escort her back to the ballroom. They parted company at the doorway and she sought out her mother, who was happily occupied in a discussion of bridal clothes at one end of the room.

"Lydia, my love," her mother said. "There you are! Where have you been?"

"Talking with an acquaintance," Lydia said, forcing a smile to her face.

"Well, you had better not neglect your fiancé any longer," her mother said with a titter.

It seemed everyone was happy about this betrothal except her and Robert.

Her fiancé appeared at her elbow.

"Lydia, my dear," Robert said, putting a proprietary hand at the small of her back. "My mother would like to introduce you to some of my cousins."

"How delightful," Lydia said, smiling.

Her jaws were *aching* from so much strained smiling.

Lydia hoped she was replying suitably to the introductions, for she was distracted by the sight of Alexander clapping Edward on the shoulder and escorting him out of the room.

"All right, Lieutenant Whittaker," Alexander demanded. "What game are you playing with my sister-in-law?"

"Did we not just have this conversation?" Edward asked.

Alexander thrust out his chin.

"I would warn you not to trifle with me now that you do not have Lydia's skirts to hide behind."

"I am not going to meet you, Lord Blakely," Edward said with a sigh. "Lydia would never let you hear the end of it if you put a bullet through me. And I would be forced to delope because I love her too much to kill you and send her sister into deepest mourning."

"You love Lydia," Blakely scoffed. "Do you honestly expect me to believe that?"

"Believe it or not as you choose," Edward replied.

"But . . . Lady Madelyn—" Blakely stammered.

"Lady Madelyn is a beautiful young lady, and I wish her joy of whichever man she fancies, so long as it is not I."

"But Lydia is such an ordinary little thing."

"You are an idiot, Lord Blakely," Edward said. "Have you seen the way she smiles? Have you seen the way her face goes soft when she is around children? She is the sweetest lady of my acquaintance. What is Lady Madelyn to her? An empty-headed doll full of useless accomplishments."

"Good God. You mean it," Lord Blakely said blankly.

Edward rolled his eyes.

"Of *course* I mean it! If you will pardon me for saying so, you are an idiot for marrying my cousin Vanessa when Lydia is only a year younger."

"Now, see here!" Alexander said fiercely. "I will thank you not to make disparaging remarks about my wife!"

"Then I will thank *you* not to say Lydia is ordinary."

"Very well," Alexander said, trying to salvage the situation with some dignity. "I think we understand one another. But you are not to impose upon Lydia. I will not pretend to be sorry if she jilts Robert Langtry, but if she does, it must be her choice."

Edward bowed, and the gentlemen parted company.

Lord, what an evening! Edward saw his parents when he re-entered the ballroom, and barely restrained himself from running away. Of course they would be invited. They were Lydia's aunt and uncle, and in the eyes of the polite world Mrs. Langtry could hardly exclude them from the festivities.

And Lady Madelyn had gone at once to greet them, he thought in disgust.

"Good evening, Lady Madelyn," Edward said, bowing over her hand after he had greeted his parents. Since she looked at him expectantly, he had to ask her to dance.

Lady Madelyn, he could not help noticing, was not in her best looks. When the dance was over, she steered him out of the room despite his best attempts to return her to his parents.

"If you would not mind, Edward," she said coyly. "I need some fresh air."

"You have played off this trick on me before," Edward reminded her as he led her outside to the gardens and installed her with a thump on a bench. He stood two feet away from her. "Now sit there like a good girl and fan yourself."

"Well," she said, all in a huff. "You are not very gallant!"

"No. And I am not going to help you make that idiot Robert Langtry jealous."

Madelyn jumped up from the bench; her cheeks were spotted with unbecoming color.

"How *dare* you!" she shrieked, and slapped him across the face.

Annoyed, he grabbed her by her shoulders and gave her a shake as if she were an unruly child.

"Behave yourself, Madelyn, or I shall put you over my knee as someone should have done long since!"

"Unhand me! Unhand me at *once!*" she cried.

"Stop that!" Edward demanded, giving her another shake. He could cheerfully have wrung her neck. "You are not in the least danger, and you know it, you silly chit!"

"Sir!" demanded Robert Langtry in thrilling accents. "Unhand that woman!"

Edward turned around, and Langtry slapped his face with his glove.

"Oh, for God's sake!" Edward said, losing his temper. "Damn it, Langtry. You will answer to me for that! I *tried* to avoid this nonsense, but if I must put a bullet through someone, I am happy that it will be you!"

"I, sir, am considered an excellent shot," Langtry said, putting his glove back on with supercilious care.

"Fine! Name your friends!" Edward shouted. The look of gratification on Lady Madelyn's face made him itch to slap the little fool. "I hope you are happy now," he said, bowing to her.

"I will leave the two of you alone to finish enacting your little drama."

Langtry grabbed his arm to detain him, but Edward gave him a hard shove that set him reeling.

"*Enough,* Langtry. If you need time to appoint a second, just send me word. I will name Lord Blakely."

"Blakely?" Langtry said in surprise. "Since when are you so friendly with that fellow?"

"I am not, but much as I dislike him, I know he has the sense to keep his mouth shut about this affair."

"Very well, sir. You will be contacted by my second when I have appointed one."

The gentlemen bowed and parted company.

Edward went back into the ballroom, and was annoyed to find Lord Blakely sitting between Lydia and her mother.

Mrs. Whittaker gave him a frown as he approached, so his bow to her was perfunctory.

"Lord Blakely, a word with you, if you please," he said.

Lydia looked up at him, but for once he only spared her a passing glance and a little inclination of the head. Solemnly, she returned it.

"What is it?" Lord Blakely said, following Edward to a secluded little space behind a potted plant.

"I am to fight a duel, and I have named you as my second."

"You seem to have a talent for offending people tonight," Blakely said dryly. "Why me?"

"Because I have challenged your future brother-in-law."

"And you had the effrontery to call me an idiot," Blakely murmured.

"It is a deuced awkward business," Edward said, his voice testy. "That spoiled little baggage, Lady Madelyn, manipulated me into the gardens with her. Then, when I refused to let her play off her tricks on me, she started making a fuss. Of course, what must Langtry do but pop into the affair and lay his glove across my jaw."

"Awkward," Blakely murmured. "I almost did the same earlier this evening, and I do not recall any great show of enthusiasm on your part for a duel."

"Well, do not interpret this as an expression of everlasting regard, Blakely, but I would much prefer to put a bullet through Langtry than I would through you."

"How gratifying," Blakely said dryly. "All right. I will act for you, but if Lydia finds out she will tear a strip off my hide."

"And mine," Edward said ruefully. "How could I have been such a fool? But there he was, threatening me for giving the silly chit a good shake, and all I could think was, here is a man fortunate enough to be betrothed to Lydia and he was badgering me about some imagined wrong to Lady Madelyn."

He gave a weary sigh.

"He does not realize how fortunate he is," Edward said. "Lydia is worth a dozen of Madelyn, and all he sees in her is a competent mistress for his household and a substitute mother for his wards. If she marries him, poor Lydia will end up unappreciated and unloved. He will expect her to be grateful to her dying day because he was generous enough to marry her so she could solve all his problems for him."

Blakely surprised both of them very much by putting a consoling hand on Edward's shoulder.

"You have it bad, old chap," he commiserated.

"I do," Edward admitted ruefully. "No one, not even Lydia, realizes *how* bad, although I was in a fair way to convincing her until you so rudely interrupted."

"In justice, I must point out that she *is* engaged to Langtry, no matter how much we deplore it, and you *were* making her cry."

"I know. I probably would have done the same if I had found some fellow imposing on one of my sisters," Edward admitted.

"Well, I will meet with Langtry's second and try to resolve this. If he has any brains at all, he will apologize. Not that I have much hope of that, mind. I never did rate his intelligence above half."

"Nor I, if he would prefer Lady Madelyn to Lydia," he said in disgust. "Thank you, Blakely. I will go home now. I should not have come, but I could not stay away." He gave a sad little laugh. "I suppose you do not understand that."

"Better than you think," Blakely said grimly. "My father, not wanting me to marry Vanessa, told me that she had married someone else while I was at war. When I came back, I went to a ball for no better reason than to torture myself with the sight of her. God. I was never so miserable in my life. It came out all right in the end, though, and I married Vanessa a month later."

Edward smiled, but his heart was not in it.

"I do not think this is going to come out all right, Blakely," he said.

"No," Blakely said sympathetically. "I do not think so, either."

Lydia could not stand it. Edward and Alexander had left the room together, and she was terrified that they were going to renew hostilities.

She could hardly follow them, however.

"Where is your fiancé?" her mother asked, looking cross. Lydia was hardly up to the challenge of being the belle of the ball. Even at her own engagement party, she had so few partners that she sat out two out of three dances. And her prospective bridegroom had abandoned her.

"I do not know," Lydia said, watching the doorway. She gave a sigh of relief when Edward and Alexander returned, neither looking the worse for wear.

"What is *that* about, pray?" Mrs. Whittaker said, raising her eyebrows as Edward and Alexander shook hands with relative cordiality and parted company.

Edward walked up to Robert's mother, bowed over her hand, and left.

He is leaving, Lydia thought, feeling bereft.

"There is That Woman," Mrs. Whittaker observed, glaring at the opposite side of the room where Lady Margaret was talking with Lady Letitia.

After a few terse, cold words and brittle smiles for bare courtesy's sake, the warring factions of the Whittaker family had retired to opposite ends of the ballroom.

"I see," Mrs. Whittaker said, giving Lydia a straight look, "that you danced with her son."

"I have danced with most of the gentlemen at one time or another," Lydia said, knowing her cheeks were bright red.

"And only once with your fiancé," Mrs. Whittaker observed, leading back to her original question. "Did you say something to set his back up?"

Lydia gave a long-suffering sigh. She should have known that anything that had gone amiss with Robert must be *her* fault.

"I hardly exchanged a half dozen words with him," Lydia pointed out. She stood up. "I think I will go visit the children in the nursery. They should not have retired yet."

Mrs. Whittaker grasped her arm with fingers like talons.

"You will do no such thing!" she declared. "This is *your* party, and you are going to stay here and enjoy it!"

"Yes, Mother," Lydia said helplessly.

"And stop looking so Friday-faced."

"Yes, Mother," Lydia repeated, trying to smile.

Mrs. Whittaker rolled her eyes, but before she could remonstrate, Mrs. Langtry walked over to them and engaged her in conversation.

At about that time, Madelyn and Robert came in from the gardens. Madelyn's face was flushed, and she looked as if she had been crying. But she pasted a bright smile on her face and walked toward Edward's parents.

Robert, looking tortured, walked over to Lydia.

"What is wrong, Robert?" Lydia asked before she thought. Lady Madelyn, of course, she told herself disgustedly.

"Nothing, my dear," he said with a brave smile that suggested he was about to perform a necessary but unpleasant duty. "Would you like to dance?"

"Certainly," Lydia lied, as miserable as he.

When the dance was ended, Lydia found Lady Madelyn waiting to catch Robert's eye. Lydia stood watching as they walked off together.

"Did you *see* that?" Mrs. Whittaker hissed at her elbow. "She is trying to steal him out from under your very nose, and you are doing *nothing* to stop her."

"I *could* tear her hair out by the roots," Lydia suggested, raising her brows. "Or I could throw a cup of punch in her face."

Mrs. Whittaker gave her a look of disapproval.

"Do you take *nothing* seriously?" she said in a tone of long-suffering.

"A great many things," Lydia said through compressed lips. "Lady Madelyn's airs and graces do not happen to be among them."

"She is to be married to That Woman's son."

"So I have heard," Lydia said, concentrating on keeping her voice from breaking.

"He is gone," Mrs. Whittaker said with satisfaction. "Dear Alexander obviously sent him about his business."

"Good for dear Alexander," Lydia said dryly.

Mrs. Whittaker gave a huff of disapproval and flounced away, presumably to find more congenial company.

Lydia could hardly blame her.

EIGHTEEN

"He does not love you, you know," Lady Madelyn said as Lydia watched Robert walk away to say something to his mother.

"How very *kind* of you to point that out," Lydia said dryly.

"He would not be marrying you if he did not have those dreadful children to care for!"

Lady Madelyn was obviously in a high state of agitation and about to entertain Mrs. Langtry's guests with a Cheltenham tragedy. Lydia, after living with her mother, was an expert when it came to defusing hysterics.

"Keep your voice down," she said in a no-nonsense tone.

"They are going to fight a duel over me," Lady Madelyn said triumphantly. "Robert came upon us in an alcove where Lieutenant Whittaker was forcing his attentions on me—"

Lydia regarded the little troublemaker with the scorn she deserved.

"Edward forced his attentions on *you?* I hardly think so."

"You will be laughing out the other side of your mouth when one of them is dead."

"Do you mean it is true?" asked Lydia, made uneasy by Lady Madelyn's obvious conviction.

"Robert *deserves* to be dead for breaking my heart," Lady Madelyn said angrily. "As for your cousin—he is the most ungallant man on earth. I hope they kill each other. They both deserve to be dead."

Lydia grabbed Lady Madelyn's arm, and not gently.

"Stop acting like a tragedy queen and tell me what you have done," Lydia demanded.

"*I* have done nothing," she said, giving Lydia a malicious look. "Robert slapped Edward across the face with his glove for abusing me, and Edward challenged him. If you want to know anything else, ask Alexander. Your cousin named him as his second."

"Be sure I will!" Lydia said fiercely.

All of her lethargy had dropped magically away.

It might gratify Lady Madelyn to have two abysmally *stupid* men fighting over her, but Lydia was going to put a stop to it at once!

She walked right up to Alexander and demanded that he dance with her.

"Of course, my dear," he said, lifting one eyebrow. "You will excuse me, Vanessa?"

"Certainly," said Lydia's sister, looking surprised.

"All right," Lydia barked once Alexander had placed his hand gingerly on her waist. If she looked half as dangerous as she felt, he was wise to exercise caution. "What is this nonsense about a duel between Edward and Robert?"

"I might have known you would ferret out that business," he said with a sigh.

"Lady Madelyn told me. She is quite thrilled by the prospect of having two otherwise sensible men try to murder one another over her."

"So your cousin said," Alexander said glumly. "I am bound to try to get Langtry to apologize, but I doubt if he will. Actually, for all *I* care, the bloody idiots may blow each other to kingdom come."

"Do not say that," Lydia said fiercely. *"Never* say that. Is there *nothing* you can do?"

"Nothing short of tying one of them up in the stable." Alexander gave a short, unpleasant laugh. "Take that look off your face, my girl. I am going to do no such thing."

"Well," she said in disgust. "I suppose I will have to see to it myself!"

The next day, Lydia was up bright and early and knocking on the door to the Langtry town house.

"Tell Mr. Langtry that I wish to see him at once," she said to the startled maid who answered the door.

"But Miss Whittaker," said the girl. "He is not yet risen."

"Wake him up, then! This is important!"

After a few minutes, a hastily dressed Robert came to join her in the bookroom.

"Lydia?" he said, peering at her through one half-open eye. "What is the matter?"

"You are the matter, you idiot!" she snapped.

Robert took a step backward and managed to open the other eye.

"Sorry, Lydia. I am a bit fuzzy in the head this morning. Do you mind telling me what you are in such a temper about?"

"The duel," Lydia told him, averting her face from his potent breath.

"Oh, *that,*" he said sheepishly.

"I want you to send an apology to Edward at *once.*"

"See, here, Lydia," he said, profoundly shocked. "This is a matter of honor."

"Matter of honor, indeed!" she sneered. "It is a matter of that little hussy Lady Madelyn using her wiles to provoke a weak-headed, susceptible male into making a cake of himself over her."

"See here," Robert said, drawing himself up to his full height and glaring at her. "You cannot talk that way about Madelyn."

"What are you going to do?" Lydia demanded. "Challenge *me* to a duel?"

"I will not apologize to that blackguard. No gentleman would after seeing the way he was abusing a lady."

"If I know Lady Madelyn," Lydia reasoned, "she richly deserved it." She gave him a little shove. "Oh, go sleep off your excesses, Robert. It is plain that it was a mistake to appeal to your common sense."

"Uh, Lydia," he said when she had turned away. He took an involuntary step back when she turned to face him. She imagined her expression was not pretty.

"Well?" she barked.

"I am, er, sorry."

"You are sorry," she repeated blankly.

"Yes. It must have been embarrassing for you when I ignored you for half the evening last night."

Lydia gave a shrug.

"Oh, *that*. Well, we never pretended it was a love match, did we," she said dryly. "Instead of apologizing to me, I wish you would apologize to Edward and put an end to this ridiculous business."

"Absolutely not," Robert said.

"I am beginning to agree with Lady Madelyn," Lydia said, so fiercely that Robert flinched. "You deserve to be dead. Anyone as stupid as you has no reason to live."

"Madelyn said *that?*" Robert gasped, shocked.

"Just the part about you deserving to be dead. I am the one who thinks you are too stupid to live!"

He would have remonstrated further, but Lydia plopped her bonnet onto her head with a snap and left.

An hour later she was in Stoneham House demanding to see Lady Madelyn.

"Come *here,* you little wretch," she growled when Lady Madelyn appeared in the doorway, looking only half awake. She had obviously just arisen, but she was dressed in sky-blue muslin and every auburn hair was in place.

Lydia wanted to shake her like a rat.

"What on earth is wrong with you?" Madelyn said, blinking.

"Listen to me," Lydia said, grasping Madelyn's forearms until the spoiled beauty squealed. "We are going to Robert's house *right now* and you are going to make him apologize to Edward and put an end to this duel."

"Certainly not," Madelyn sniffed. "I cannot go to a man's home so early in the day. My reputation would be ruined."

"If you do not," Lydia said softly, "I am going to pull every hair out of your head."

"Oh, help! Help! She is going to murder me!" Madelyn shrieked. She smiled smugly at Lydia when a handful of servants skidded into the room. "Miss Whittaker is leaving," Madelyn said haughtily. "Show her out."

Lydia gave Madelyn a look that should have felled her where she stood, and left.

She had no choice but to talk to Edward.

"Lydia!" he exclaimed when she appeared at the door to his lodgings. His landlady gave a sniff in Lydia's direction, making it plain that young ladies forward enough to call on gentlemen were no better than they should be.

"She'll not come in," the landlady said, peering at them both through narrowed eyes. "I shan't have any of *that* in *my* house."

"We will walk across the street and have our conversation on the sidewalk," Edward said, taking Lydia's arm and escorting her away before Lydia could renew hostilities with the landlady. He laughed, and Lydia rounded on him. "None of that, my girl," he said. "To what do I owe the honor of this visit?"

"To your own everlasting stupidity, you great clod," Lydia said fervently.

Edward's jaw dropped.

"I beg your pardon?" he said.

"I found out about the duel," she replied.

"Who told you?" he demanded, taking her shoulders and shaking her until her bonnet fell off and was hanging by its strings.

"Madelyn, of course," Lydia said. "People are staring, Edward."

"Oh. Sorry," he said sheepishly, releasing her.

"You should have seen her, all swollen up with conceit because she had provoked a pair of idiots to fight a duel for her honor."

"Well, maybe Langtry is fighting for her honor," Edward said bitterly. "I am fighting for the sheer joy of putting a bullet through the silly ass."

"If he apologizes, will you accept?"

"Of course I will accept," Edward said with a bitter laugh. "He forced a quarrel on me in a weak moment—I was trying to strangle Lady Madelyn at the time. She was deliberately using me to make your darling Robert jealous, and I had just about had enough of stubborn females."

Lydia gave him a shamefaced look.

"That means me, I suppose."

"Definitely," he said, putting his arm around her. "Darling, if he manages to get in a lucky shot and kill me, promise me you will break off your engagement to him."

"Break off my engagement to him?" Lydia said, her eyes hard. "If he kills you, I will *murder* him!"

"That is my girl," Edward said proudly. "What an army wife you would make."

"*Stop* it," Lydia told him when he tilted her chin up.

"Humor a man who might be facing death tomorrow," he murmured, just before he kissed her.

"Tomorrow!" Lydia squeaked, pushing him away. "The duel is tomorrow? I have not much time, Edward. I have to leave."

With that, she straightened her bonnet, gave him a quick kiss on his startled lips, and ran down the street to the hackney carriage she had kept waiting for her.

It was dawn on Primrose Hill, and the gentlemen had already started pacing.

Edward sighed and thought of Lydia as he looked straight

ahead into the rosy sunrise. Would it be the last one he would see?

Lydia, he thought. At least he knew she would not marry Langtry if he managed to kill him. She had promised. It was not much consolation, but it was something.

His senses seemed to be heightened.

Edward could hear the waking birds calling. He could smell the grass and flowers. There was a slight chill in the air that accorded well with his mood.

He turned and prepared to fire, seeing that Langtry, dressed in a long black frock coat and wearing a grim look on his face, was already facing him.

This was it, then, Edward thought, surprising himself by being calm.

The rest of the drama appeared to unfold very slowly. Perhaps Edward was already a little mad. He could see Langtry's look of concentration as he took aim.

But time suddenly snapped back to its usual pace when Lydia ran between them.

"Stop it! Stop it this instant!" she shrieked.

"Christ, Lydia!" shouted Edward, terrified, as he grabbed her and pushed her to the ground. He threw his own body over hers to shield her. Langtry stifled an oath and jerked his arm up so his bullet would miss both of them.

"Here, stop that!" Lydia cried, sounding pained as she pushed at Edward. "Robert may shoot you, but he is not about to shoot *me!*"

"Do not be so sure," said Langtry caustically from above them as he regarded his childhood friend with disfavor. He was breathless from running. "What the devil do you think you are about, Lydia?"

Edward got to his feet and put his hand down to assist Lydia. He tried to brush some grass off her skirt, but she slapped his hands away.

"That will *do,* Edward," she said sternly. "Thank you," she added in a dignified voice as he passed her crushed hat to her. She fixed Langtry with a stare that made him flinch. "I am putting an end to this stupid duel, of course."

"See here!" Langtry said when a uniformed soldier took his arm.

Edward found another at his elbow.

He had been so intent on Lydia that he had not noticed she was not alone.

"Lydia," Robert said accusingly. *"Tell* me you did not lay information against us."

"Certainly I did," she said crisply.

She and Robert both gave Edward a forbidding glare when he burst into laughter and could not seem to stop.

"If you are quite through," she said disapprovingly when he gasped to a halt.

"Quite," he said meekly.

"Gentlemen," one of the soldiers began, taking Langtry's arm and starting to draw him away.

"Very *good,* Lydia," Edward said out of the side of his mouth. "How do you suggest we handle *this* little difficulty?"

"You and Robert are both men of fortune," she said, giving him that exasperated do-I-have-to-think-of-everything look that women seemed to excel in. "Bribe them."

Alexander interrupted Edward's indignant response.

"Here, Lieutenant Whittaker," Blakely said, his dark eyes bright with amusement. "I will just have a word with the officers, if you will excuse me. Lieutenant Rogers, is that you?"

"Lord Blakely! Do not tell me *you* have something to do with this business," the soldier said, following Blakely when he gestured for him to step aside with him.

Langtry gave Lydia a stern look.

"Lydia, I am surprised at you. Laying information about a duel! Have you no sense of propriety?"

"Apparently not," she said dryly.

"I have never heard of such a thing," Robert said, shaking his head in disbelief.

"Well, cheer up, old thing," she said. "Console yourself with the knowledge that our betrothal is at an end, or it will be by the time we have informed our mothers and society at large that we have agreed we will not suit."

"But Lydia—" Robert objected.

"No need to fly into the boughs," Lydia said, laying a hand on his arm. "I shall take it all on my own head and be branded a heartless jilt."

"But—"

"You heard the lady," Edward said, stepping in front of Langtry when he would have taken Lydia's arm.

"You stay out of this, you—" Langtry began.

"Stop it!" Lydia said through gritted teeth. "Or you will be challenging one another to another duel!" She pointed her finger at Langtry. "I am not marrying you, so there is an end to it!"

"Good girl," said Edward approvingly.

"And *you,"* she said, turning on him. "If you ever challenge anyone to a duel again, I will—"

"What?" he asked, enjoying the way her cheekbones glowed with color and her eyes shot sparks. "Give me a kiss, love."

Lydia blinked, but before she could reply to this outrageous request, Alexander returned to them and the soldiers started to leave.

"What did you say to them?" Lydia asked.

"Fortunately, Lieutenant Rogers was an officer in my old regiment. I persuaded him that this was all a silly misunderstanding and thereby saved you both a tremendous fine." He nodded to a man in a black suit carrying a leather bag. "Let us go to breakfast. I am starving. I will just see Lydia off in my carriage, and—"

"See Lydia off!" Lydia said indignantly. "You think you are going to bundle me into a carriage and send me home after *this?* I missed my breakfast and *I* am starving, too."

Langtry looked shocked, but Edward laughed and put an arm around her waist.

"My love, I am going to buy you the biggest, rarest sirloin in London," he promised.

When they arrived at the pub, the proprietor gave Lydia a disapproving look, but Edward returned it with a stare that dared him to say a disparaging word about the presence of a lady at their table.

Soon an ecstatic Edward was slicing pieces of rare beef from an enormous sirloin as fast as Lydia could eat them.

"What a woman," Edward said admiringly. "Who would have thought you would be clever enough to lay information against us to stop the duel."

"It was *not* the action of a lady," Robert sniffed.

"Oh, take a damper, Langtry," Edward said scornfully. "Is it my fault you have appalling taste in women? Lydia, darling, you *must* marry me."

Lydia started to cough. Edward pounded her smartly on the back. Alexander looked up in concern from his eggs, but when he saw that Lydia was drawing in air without difficulty, he waved the doctor back to the seat from which he had hastily arisen and went back to his meal.

"There you go, love. Breathe," Edward said soothingly as he massaged Lydia's neck. "All right now?"

"Yes," Lydia said in a husky voice. "Really, Edward. You cannot ask me to marry you while I am swallowing. I could have choked to death!"

"I beg your pardon, my dear. What is your answer?"

"Well, our mothers will put up a dreadful din," Lydia pointed out. "And you know your father and grandfather will probably disinherit you."

"Our mothers will soon find something else to complain about, and we will still have my pay as an officer. It is not much," he admitted, "but if any woman can stretch it to cover the essentials, you can."

"True," Lydia conceded as she took another bite of beef. "Pass me the bread, will you, Alexander?"

"Certainly, Lydia," her brother-in-law said, handing her the plate.

Robert made a strangled sound and buried his head in his hands.

"Was it something we said, Langtry?" Edward asked, regarding the distressed gentleman with a smug look. "It is probably not in the best of taste for me to propose to your former fiancée so soon after you have been jilted, but buck up, old man. There are scores of excessively silly females in London, and one of them is bound to take a fancy to you."

Lydia gave Edward a frown and batted him on the shoulder.

"Robert, your eggs are getting cold," Lydia observed.

Langtry regarded Lydia with a look akin to pity.

"You are the most indelicate female I have ever met," he said sadly.

"Edward, darling, sit down," Lydia said casually, signaling Alexander to hand her the teapot. "You cannot go around challenging every gentleman who says something unflattering about me, particularly when it is true." She glanced at Langtry. "Finish your breakfast, Robert. It is a pity to waste good food."

"Here, have mine," Langtry said with a reluctant smile as he handed Lydia his plate. She gave a snort of amusement. "If you will all excuse me, I have a call to make."

"He is going to call on Lady Madelyn, I suppose," Lydia said, wrinkling her nose. She turned to Edward and smiled brilliantly at him. "Yes," she added.

"Yes?" Edward repeated in some confusion.

"Yes, I will marry you," Lydia said.

"Lydia! Darling!" Edward shouted ecstatically. He broke off and looked away from Lydia's enraptured face.

"What the devil is the matter with them?" he asked crossly as Alexander, Robert's second, and the doctor burst into laughter.

NINETEEN

"I have nursed a viper in my bosom," cried Mrs. Whittaker, fumbling for her vinaigrette. She put her hand to her head and tottered a little for dramatic effect.

"Here, Mama," Lydia said soothingly as she located the vial of smelling salts and held it under her afflicted parent's nose until her eyes watered.

"Stop that," Mrs. Whittaker snapped. "I *forbid* it, I tell you!"

Alexander appeared in the doorway and stood propped in it with his arms crossing his chest and a rueful expression on his face.

"There you are, Lydia," he said. "You have broken the news to your mother, I see."

"Alexander!" cried Mrs. Whittaker. "Perhaps *you* can talk some sense into this headstrong girl!"

"Highly unlikely," Alexander said, patting his mother-in-law on the shoulder. "It seems she is in love with the fellow, and he with her."

"No!"

"I am afraid so," Alexander said. "We may as well give in with good grace. If we do not, they will elope, and you know how much Aggie and Amy were counting on a wedding."

Mrs. Whittaker threw up her hands.

"I suppose you are right," she said, giving Lydia a look of disgust. "Very well. I shall give my consent. But only because there is no sense in wasting a perfectly good bridal gown, mind!"

"Thank you, Mother," Lydia said, kissing her on the cheek. "This means so much to me! Edward's father will disinherit him, I am sure, because Lady Margaret will insist upon it. It would be too hard for us to be alienated from you as well."

"That dreadful woman," Mrs. Whittaker said, looking a bit cheered. "I would give a pocketful of gold guineas to see how *she* is taking the news."

Alexander patted his mother-in-law's hand. "With nowhere near the grace with which *you* have accepted it, I am certain," he said fondly. "Motherly affection will always guide your tender heart. We can only pity Lieutenant Whittaker for having such a mother."

Lydia rolled her eyes at Alexander, certain that he had gone too far. But Mrs. Whittaker obviously accepted this florid praise as her due.

"One cannot expect That Woman to put her child's happiness before her own vain ambition," she gloated. "She will be positively livid!"

"I will not have it, I tell you," Lady Margaret screeched when Edward told his parents the news. "Henry!" she cried, turning to her husband for support. *"Tell* him!"

"Uh, son," Henry Whittaker said obediently, "I am obliged to tell you that if you marry your cousin Lydia, I will disinherit you in your brother William's favor."

"And I will see that Papa disinherits you, too!" Lady Margaret said, jutting her lower lip out. "My son will *not* marry *That Woman's* daughter."

"Mother, I am very much afraid I *will* because I cannot live without her," Edward said calmly, patting Lady Margaret's shoulder. "Do not worry. You will grow to love Lydia in time."

Lady Margaret gave a huff of indignation at this outrageous statement.

"Never," she said in accents of pure loathing.

"Now, Mother," Edward said heartily. "Lydia is a wonderful girl. Strong. Spirited. Passionate. Determined. Reminds me of you."

While his mother sputtered incoherently at this new outrage, Edward smiled blandly at his father's horrified expression.

"I mean it about the fortune, Edward," Mr. Whittaker said.

"I know. It makes no difference," Edward told him.

"But she is your first cousin! You know the Church frowns on such marriages," his father said.

"Nonsense. First cousins marry all the time."

"Only to consolidate family fortunes," Mr. Whittaker said impatiently. "There is no fortune involved here!"

"No, indeed," Edward agreed with a sunny smile. "William is to be congratulated."

"Edward!" shrieked his mother. "What about Lady Madelyn?"

"She will have Langtry, I expect," Edward said, shaking his head. "I do not know which of them I pity more. If she comes to her senses, we can always introduce her to William."

"Are they here as guests or to keep the peace?" Lydia whispered to Edward after Alexander handed her over to him with a flourish in front of the altar.

Edward grinned and followed her glance to the pew behind them, where his fellow officers from the 10th Hussars watched the ceremony.

"Both. You look lovely."

Lydia felt her cheeks turn pink with pleasure, and she realized that she felt truly beautiful for the first time in her life. The white silk dress trimmed with silver was exquisite. She adored the feel of the tulle veil against her shoulders.

They were being married at her old parish church in Yorkshire as Lydia had wished, and although Alexander had raised his eyebrows at such an uncharacteristic desire for extravagance on Lydia's part, the aisle was banked with pink, white, and yellow roses on both sides near the front.

Edward's eyes fastened on her lips as if he intended to kiss her. The clergyman cleared his throat pointedly and began the ceremony. Lydia's senses were intoxicated with the perfume of the roses mingled with the scent of melting beeswax candles. She feared for a moment of panic that this was a dream and she would wake up.

She glanced at her three younger sisters, who were dressed in matching blue gowns with white flowers in their hair. Aggie was already fidgeting, and Mary Ann hissed dire threats about what she was going to do to her if she would not be *still*.

Lydia smiled. It was no dream.

When the minister invited the congregation to voice their objections now or forever hold their peace, Lydia felt Edward tighten his grip on her hand. To her relief, no one said anything. She would not have put it past her mother to speak up.

At last the ceremony was over, and Lydia and Edward turned to face the overflowing mass of people. Everyone in her old neighborhood was here to see her married, and the congregation included many of their families' acquaintances from London as well. Lydia knew that the gossips derived much amusement from what they called the Battle of the Mothers-in-Law, and invitations to the wedding were prized almost as much as tickets to Almack's. No doubt the attendees were hoping for a hair-pulling match between the mothers. Lydia would not be surprised if the ladies obliged them once the toasts were drunk.

"I wish you very happy, Lydia," Robert said when he reached her in the receiving line. He started to kiss her, but Edward's glare apparently made him think better of it.

"Thank you, Robert," she said before she bent and gave each of his nieces and nephews a kiss.

As they walked away, little Matthew turned around to look at Lydia with sad eyes, until Robert bent to speak soothingly to him and lead him away. She knew that Robert's petition to Madelyn's guardian for her hand in marriage had been refused, and so his wards would be motherless for a good while longer.

"They will be all right, Lydia," Edward whispered into Lydia's ear. "I am not fond of Langtry, but even I can see that he is an affectionate and loving uncle."

Lydia's heart swelled with love. Edward always knew what she was thinking.

Then Edward's parents came face-to-face with them. A hush fell over the bystanders.

"Mother! Father! I am so pleased you decided to come," Edward exclaimed joyfully.

Lady Margaret's jaw was set, but she kissed her son on the cheek. She took Lydia's hand and released it without quite looking at her.

Mr. Whittaker gave his wife a pointed look.

"We want you to have the house in Yorkshire as a wedding gift," she said grudgingly. "It will be yours free and clear. The papers are drawn up and awaiting Edward's signature whenever it is convenient for him to sign."

Lydia gasped.

"Lady Margaret! Mr. Whittaker! How *very* kind and generous of you," she exclaimed. She would live in her old home with the man she loved. Not even in her most extravagant dreams would she have dared imagine this.

"Well, you must live *somewhere,* and it is a sad, rubbishing place, after all," Lady Margaret told her, obviously embarrassed by the sentimentality that had prompted her and her husband to make this gesture of goodwill. "We still intend to disinherit you, mind," she added quickly, just so there would be no misunderstanding.

"I know, Mother," Edward said gravely. Lady Margaret gave

him a brisk nod, took her husband's arm, and stepped away quickly.

"Take that look off your face, Love," Edward said to Lydia as he escorted her out into the morning sunlight. "The delight of having you as my wife is worth the loss of a hundred fortunes. Give us that beautiful smile of yours or everyone will think you regret the deed now that it is done."

Lydia felt happy tears fill her eyes as she and her husband walked through the crossed swords of the Prince of Wales's Own Royal 10th Hussars and into their new life.

About the Author

Kate Huntington lives with her family in Illinois. She is the author of two Zebra Regency romances and is currently working on her third, which will be published in July, 2000. Kate loves to hear from her readers and you may write to her c/o Zebra Books. Please include a self-addressed stamped envelope if you wish a response.

BOOK YOUR PLACE ON OUR WEBSITE
AND MAKE THE
READING CONNECTION!

We've created a customized website just for our very special readers, where you can get the inside scoop on everything that's going on with Zebra, Pinnacle and Kensington books.

When you come online, you'll have the exciting opportunity to:

- View covers of upcoming books
- Read sample chapters
- Learn about our future publishing schedule (listed by publication month *and author*)
- Find out when your favorite authors will be visiting a city near you
- Search for and order backlist books from our online catalog
- Check out author bios and background information
- Send e-mail to your favorite authors
- Meet the Kensington staff online
- Join us in weekly chats with authors, readers and other guests
- Get writing guidelines
- AND MUCH MORE!

**Visit our website at
http://www.zebrabooks.com**